# CHANCE ENCOUNTER
## ❧ BOOK THREE ❧

### A PRIDE & PREJUDICE RE-IMAGINING

# NEY MITCH

CHANCES FADE
Copyright © 2022 by Ney Mitch

ISBN: 978-1-955784-77-1

Published by Satin Romance
An Imprint of Melange Books, LLC
White Bear Lake, MN 55110
www.satinromance.com

Published in the United States of America.

Cover Design by Caroline Andrus

# DEDICATION & AUTHOR'S NOTE

Readers, we have arrived at the third book in the series, and you are delightful for reading this far!

Once more, you are the ones that I dedicate this series to, as well as my family, publisher, and all the other talented individuals who have worked on this series.

Now, without further ado, let's begin, shall we?

And never will I forget that Helyn Roberts-Vickers is willing to support this series to the very end. A special dedication to you.

Ney Mitch

# PROLOGUE

## DARCY'S COUSIN

*R*iding along the streets of Brighton in his carriage, Mr. John Darcy tapped his hand against his lap, nervously. Indeed, this was the last way that he wished to spend the day, but since his brother had no stomach for the situation, Mr. John Darcy was put in the difficult position of having to save his niece from utter ruin.

This scandal was the last thing that their family needed. It also rendered his late brother's opinion of his little brother's ability to do anything right as valid.

Mr. John Darcy was the youngest of three brothers. The eldest, the late Mr. Darcy of Pemberley, naturally inherited everything, as was the eldest son's right. The younger brothers had the misfortune of being born the second and last, therefore, they had to make their way in the world.

Rather than accepting their less than generous lot in life, the younger brothers executed the only thing that they could: hold their oldest brother in contempt for it, inspired by the jealousy that raged within them.

When they were children, the three brothers were friendly and enjoyed the bonds of sibling loyalty, but as they aged, the difference in their situations in life became known to them. The two youngest Darcy sons realized that they had to take professions and would be relatively poor all their lives if they did not support themselves. The concept of having to work for their living, or marry a very wealthy woman, was too much for their sensibilities and they felt very ill-used. Taking the tragedy of their lives to heart, they never forgave the eldest Darcy brother for his luck in being born first.

But this is not what led to the ultimate discord between all three sons. No. It was merely the beginning in a long line of offenses being committed on all three sides. Mr. William Darcy, who had been close to his two brothers when they were children, could not abide the rift that occurred as they aged. Seeing his younger brothers grumble as he walked past them had led to Mr. William Darcy inevitably hating them back.

But Mr. William Darcy's fortune triumphed over them both in another fashion. Being the eldest son, ladies in the ton were naturally drawn toward him. In particular, a lovely, wealthy woman named Miss Anne Fitzwilliam. Beautiful, lively, and having a dowry of sixty thousand pounds, she was the perfect woman for the two younger brothers. The second Darcy brother, Mr. Lionel Darcy, fell in love with her and made attempts to court her. He was almost successful at convincing her to take an interest in him until his older brother saw her.

Like his younger brother, Mr. William Darcy fell victim to love at first sight. And Miss Anne Fitzwilliam returned his attentions. For not only was Mr. William Darcy the eldest, but he had been blessed with the best features and figure between the three sons. He also was the best at conversation.

Needless to say, his younger brother, Mr. Lionel Darcy, was enraged. After his older brother's marriage to Anne Fitzwilliam, the two men never spoke again. Mr. Lionel Darcy found his heiress, married her, and learned to hate her soon into the marriage. After all, how happy can a wedding be without taking the pains to find something about your spouse agreeable? One daughter came out of the union: Miss Elena Darcy. Growing up in a household where neither mother nor father liked each other, would naturally have affected the girl. They showed some affection to her, but not as much as any child deserves. This left a marked impression on her. As she aged, Miss Elena Darcy was so repulsed at her parents' treatment of each other, that she learned a different lesson than what they expected. She *was resolved* to never be like them. She *was resolved* to marry for love and never turn into the bitter creatures that they were. And that was what led to her present situation...

---

As Mr. John Darcy's carriage turned a corner, there was a set of soldiers in their regimentals, being a little roused as they passed his carriage. One of them banged their hand against his carriage's side. Mr. John Darcy rolled his eyes and grumbled.

"Officers!" He groaned. "Give a man a redcoat and he forgets that he is next to no importance."

Soon, he reached an affluent hotel, exited the carriage, went to the front desk, and requested to be shown to Miss Elena Darcy's room. Upon getting there, he knocked on the door, fearing this confrontation.

After all? How do you meet your niece who has run away to elope with someone?

No servant opened the door, but rather it was Elena Darcy herself. Possessing the same Darcy elegance and beauty, her hair was a dark brown, her eyes were blue, her face was round, and she was of medium height. When seeing her Uncle John, she breathed a sigh of relief.

"Uncle John," she extolled, taking his hand, and encouraging him to come in, "thank goodness! I am happy to see you."

Seeing her so desirous for help softened his heart and he felt all his speeches on immorality give way and give in.

"And I am happy to see that you are well, my dear," he assured her as she closed the door behind them. Standing there, looking at her, he saw that she was bearing her situation as best that one may.

"Well, Elena," he began, "I do not know whether to scold you for getting yourself into this situation, or to praise you for bearing this all with such strength."

"What I have done, I admit to it, and you do not have to mince words with me: father is still upset with me, isn't he?"

Uncle John Darcy looked down at his hands, folding them in front of him.

His silence said it all. Elena moved away from her uncle and sat down by the fire.

"So, the question is now me, isn't it?" Elena asked. "It's about what are you all going to do with me and the scandal that will ensue?"

"That scandal still can be remedied by you," he insisted, sitting down. "I have heard the particulars, and it seems like the man that you ran away with is willing to marry you."

"He is more married to the idea of my money than really interested in marrying me," Elena retorted. "When we first arrived in London together, he said that we stopped there simply to inform his relatives that we were going to Gretna Green. Then I stumbled upon a letter in his purse that he was going to send father, claiming that he will marry me, expecting my father to supply me with a large dowry. The implication was clear: he was telling my father that if he supplied me with a large amount of money, he would marry me and make sure that no scandal would arise. He was charming, and he deceived me. I believed myself to be in love, but all the while, he was acting on bribery, blackmail and being mercenary."

"And your father is willing to give you all your dowry and much more for the marriage to take place."

"My father has now only one concern: avoiding scandal. He has never cared for my happiness."

"Now, Elena, come now…"

"He loves me because he is obliged to. But like my late mother, there was always a distance there. As well as there being a distance here. It has not escaped my notice that he sent you to talk to me, because he cannot bear the sight of me. He is more concerned with covering up the fracas than of my happiness. For how could he expect me to marry a man who is clearly a fortune hunter?"

Mr. John Darcy was appalled with her attitude toward it all.

"I am ashamed of you, Elena!" He gasped, standing up. "Do you not see that you got yourself caught up in this?"

Elena looked away from him and into the fire, preparing for a speech where she was informed how she let everyone down, and lacked any sense of self-contempt.

"You were the one who ran off with a worthless libertine, becoming prey to his wanton ways, allowed yourself to be deceived, and then were shocked when you discovered that you were wrong about everything. So, you left him immediately and now live in a hotel, on your father's account."

"I could not stay one moment longer in the house of that man!" Elena spat.

"The man that you ran away with. That abominable officer, who uses his redcoat to hide his deceptive nature. Oh, and what was his name?"

"Mr. James Wilson," Elena clarified, "and that will be the last time that I utter that. After this hour, I am determined to never mention his name again."

"But don't you see?" he countered. "You are determined to forget the experience and act like it never happened. Our name and fortune do not buy you the excuse to forget your past actions and erase them. But rather, our family's reputation—"

"Yes, I know," Elena cut in, "we are Darcys, and our family cannot abide any sort of scandal. For if we do, then the sophisticated thing would be for us to banish the person who caused the scandal from our family. Believe me, I have no intention of forgetting my past actions, but nor am I going to walk the halls weeping and pretending to be the fragile woman when I am not. My mistake was committed days ago, and I am determined to move on from that instant. But I will not do it by marrying Mr. Wilson. He fooled me once, so shame on him. But to fool me twice, then shame upon me. I will not be shamed twice, nor will I pretend to be a delicate creature. I mean to move on from all this."

"If you don't marry Mr. Wilson," Mr. John Darcy persisted, "then rumor will spread of your flight with him, I assure you."

"I will face it all in my own way," Elena persisted, "and I was hoping that my family would forgive and support me in all this, but now my father is not speaking to me. Therefore, you are one of the sources that I appeal to. Uncle, Father may not wish to speak to me now, but I want to believe that you are kinder to me. Can I stay with you at your estate, Holden Hall, until this scandal ends? Soon, people will not care about my scandal, one way or the other, because they will find something else to talk about. Therefore, will you help me? Can I stay with you and Aunt Agnes?"

Mr. John Darcy's eyes widened in alarm.

---

This request clearly was not what Mr. John Darcy was expecting. He was, as he reasoned, a perfectly proper sort of gentleman: the sort whose familial affection only spread far enough to send gifts at Christmas, agree to attend fancy dinners and large parties, but never exert himself to anything that would inconvenience his life.

He did love his niece, but in the way that he was raised to love: logically and not always emotionally. Therefore, the very concept of taking in his unfortunate niece had presented two images in his mind:

First, they were family, and she wished for help. His chivalrous side was stirred to assist.

Second, yes, they were family, but her coming to stay with them was the worst possible thing he could imagine. Especially since he worried that her presence would cause a corruption for his daughters. And therein was the solution to his dilemma.

He wanted to help his niece, but his daughters' safety and security from scandal was paramount—and this was how his logical mind worked.

Looking uneasy, he mumbled something that was incoherent.

"Sorry, uncle," Elena pressed, "I did not understand what you just said."

Fumbling about, he decided that he had to come straight to the point.

"My poor niece," he began, "my poor *poor* niece! You know that I care for your welfare and that I pity your state. But right now, my eldest daughter is involved in a courtship to Sir Ellington's son, and the other daughter has just come out. I worry that having any scandal in their home might hurt their chances at obtaining such matches. I shall do everything in my power to help you, but having you stay at Holden Hall is quite out of the question."

Elena was not perturbed by this at all. In fact, she had known that this would be her uncle's reply the entire time. Their family was one that had great pride in the Darcy name, but that pride often slipped into vanity. Their chief aim in life was maintaining a good name, and their self-consequence turned into being a little too occupied with how they were viewed. Elena always despised this, because it may have led to outward popularity, but behind closed doors, it led to familial emptiness and intolerance to human frailty. Therefore, Elena was not surprised that her uncle's wishes for her good fortune would only extend so far as words, but not with actions.

"I understand and sympathize with your predicament, Uncle," Elena replied, confidently and unaffected. "After all, your daughters —and my cousins—happiness in marriage is paramount. And the men that court them may have deep affection for them, but not so much so that they can weather my cousins' connections to me. Their unfortunate relationship to me would ruin my cousins forever, and those men have no choice but to abandon all hope— yes, these are the right sort of men for my cousins to marry."

"Your thoughtfulness does you credit," Mr. John Darcy said, relieved.

Elena briefly closed her eyes, amazed at her uncle's stupidity.

"And as such," Elena continued, "I took the liberty of considering another alternative."

"Oh," Mr. John Darcy said, surprised and with his eyebrow raised. "What alternative do you speak of?"

Elena stood up, went over to a desk, and took out a letter.

"I have written to another relative of ours."

"Who?"

"My other cousins. Mr. Fitzwilliam Darcy and Miss Georgiana of Pemberley."

When hearing this, Mr. John Darcy was overcome, to say the least. His face distorted and he looked as if he was in the midst of an apoplectic fit. He fumbled around as he stood in place, shocked.

"Calm yourself, uncle," Elena advised. "It is only a letter."

"A letter?" He gasped. "A letter to your cousins?!"

"Yes."

"The cousins of my late brother."

"Yes, Uncle John."

"The brother who went to his grave with a feud between him and your father."

"Yes, my late uncle, Mr. Darcy."

"You wish to connect with his children?"

"Yes."

"The cousins that you have never met a day in your life?"

"Actually, that part of the story is complicated."

"How so?"

"Oh, Uncle John, there is no reason that you have to trouble yourself," Elena urged, "first, I have not sent the letter yet, so I do not know if they will accept my request. Especially since I do not care about the feud that my father had with his older brother. For just because two brothers despised each other to the bitter end, does not mean that their children ought to do so. Since I have nowhere else to go, I shall take my chances."

"Your father will be very angry that you went to your uncle's children."

"As I am angry that my father will not let me into his home now that I am disgraced. He has put me into this desperate action. If this door is closed to me, then I will have nowhere to go. Therefore, pray for me, uncle. Pray that the current Mr. Darcy of Pemberley and his sister, Georgiana, are willing to have enough compassion to overcome any doubts that they have on that score."

"Elena, I urge you," Mr. John Darcy pleaded, "do not send that letter."

"My situation urges me to. I am short of friends, and I need them, now more than ever. I never valued the idea of not knowing my cousins just because you three brothers have let the apple of discord occur for so long. So, I esteem you, Uncle John. But in this case, I shall be guided by my own reason."

Mr. John Darcy stood up and paced back and forth. At last, he picked up his hat.

"And there is nothing I can do to convince you otherwise?"

"Forgive me, uncle, but I am adamant."

Resigned, he put on his hat and cloak.

"Very well," he said, "I pity you, Elena. I was hoping, when I came, I could convince you to be reasonable."

"With all my heart, I also had made wishes on how our meeting would result, and I can say that I know how disappointed you must feel."

With that, Mr. John Darcy left. Elena called in the servant and ordered the letter to be sent.

When alone, Miss Elena Darcy sat down and looked out the window, concerned.

"Georgiana," she said to herself, "I hope that I was not deceived in you."

# CHAPTER 1

## GOOD LORD!

*I*t felt like a moment of social doom.

In the sitting room, Mr. Darcy, Kitty, Georgiana, and I were standing there, watching the scene of Mr. Bingley and Colonel Fitzwilliam standing before Jane, each wishing to propose.

Both men were adamant.

Both men were desiring to be the first to offer their proposal.

Leaning into Mr. Darcy, I was not intending to meet this scene as nothing more than a bystander.

"We must do something."

"Quite right," he whispered back, venomous, "I will not have awkwardness ruin our most special day."

Stepping forward, Mr. Darcy let his imposing nature fill up the room.

"Announcements?" He began. "How fortuitous to mention it and how clever of you both. By mentioning that, you have reminded me of some news that I wish to acquaint you both with. Today, I can announce one of the happiest things has occurred to me. Miss Elizabeth and I have realized that we both could not spend another day being anything else but greatly attached. Miss Elizabeth Bennet and I are engaged to be married, and I would like both of your well-wishes on the subject."

This had the desired effect!

Both Mr. Bingley and Colonel Fitzwilliam flinched, then recovered and rallied their spirits.

"Good lord," Mr. Bingley began, breathy, "I had not the slightest notion that your affection had reached such a pitch. Thank goodness for it! Congratulations."

"Congratulations indeed," Colonel Fitzwilliam added, shifting his look away from Mr. Bingley. "I am happy that you both finally have come to your senses and realized that you are perfect for each other. Miss Elizabeth, I do not believe that there is any woman more worthy of my cousin than you."

"Thank you, Colonel." I gave him a pleasant smile.

This gave Jane time to breathe out, happy to know that the attention had been deflected from her.

"And it adds to something that I said from the very beginning," Mr. Bingley compiled, "remember, Darcy? When we first met the Miss Bennets at the assembly dance. I pointed Miss Elizabeth out to you and said she was very agreeable. Did I not?"

"Yes, you did," Mr. Darcy responded, "and I should have heeded your advice in that moment."

"Imagine if you had?" I asked, with a wickedness to my eye. "It could have all turned out differently from the beginning. But it didn't. Ah well, we may not have connected at the start, but we found each other in the end."

"And I believe that I am the better for it. Now let us celebrate and have some punch."

Georgiana ordered a servant to bring us some refreshments and we all sat down.

"The situation of this all is most wonderful," Kitty added, hoping to ease the tension in the room as well. "For you must understand what it is like for us sisters. We went into this circumstance thinking that we knew how everything was to end. And it didn't. Mr. Darcy, I do not deny that when I first met you, I had never believed that you would ever consider becoming a part of our family, or rather, making us a part of yours. I am happy to be wrong."

"I can very well believe that you thought so initially," Mr. Darcy added, "for when I came to Hertfordshire with Mr. Bingley's family, I was very much out of humour and was above being pleased by anything."

"Ah yes," Mr. Bingley added. "I remember that very well. Soon, I got the feeling that you would never find one full day of happiness until you left Hertfordshire. And now, to know that you had found joy the entire time. I flatter myself that the best thing I had ever done was the last thing you wanted me to do, Darcy: rent Netherfield Park."

"I never disapproved of the home, but of the company in the town," Mr. Darcy clarified. "But in that way, I was in error. And I find my desire to walk down memory lane. Forgive me, Richard, but when a man gets engaged, he wishes to recall all the moments that led up to it."

"Oh, please do tell us all from the very beginning," Georgiana encouraged. "I cannot help but be curious about it."

"Well, I am all for it," Mr. Bingley supported, "since I was there from the very beginning, but was blind as to what was going on under my very nose."

"I confess that I am of the same mind," Kitty added, "for I was there as well, and saw not a bit of affection in the case. They left us both in the dark for some time."

"Because we ourselves were in the dark," I explained. "Mr. Darcy and I fell into love in the oddest of ways. We both seemed to have been in the middle of it before we even knew we began. Oh dear." I turned to Mr. Darcy. "Am I making assumptions and speaking for us both?"

"I am only amazed that you are correct," Mr. Darcy responded, with a hint of a smile. "That is precisely how it happened for me. First, I was successful at resisting your charms, and then the next thing I know, I am wishing to always have you at my side. It was very frustrating."

"I know the feeling," I empathized, "for, one moment, I am despising your 'indifference and contempt' of me, and then the next moment, I wished to befriend you and always know what you were thinking."

"There really is a story here," Colonel Fitzwilliam observed.

"Yes," Kitty answered, "and you must humor those of us who like a long love story."

"I shall give way to everyone's wishes," the Colonel conceded, "and I submit my sword and surrender to your pleas."

"As long as you promise not to use our story for your book," I pointed out, "then we shall confess all."

"Book?" Mr. Bingley asked.

"Ah yes," Jane finally spoke up—this had been the first time that she spoke since both men arrived. "Kitty has just told us some very wonderful news."

"Well," Kitty said with a smile, her face aglow with lively childishness. "It perhaps is only wonderful to myself because I find pleasure in it. But perhaps I will prove to have no talent in it at all and therefore all will come to nothing. Over these last couple of years, I have been attempting to be a writer."

Mr. Bingley and Colonel Fitzwilliam leaned forward without knowing it.

"What?" they both said, in unison. This unified speech disconcerted both men, and they looked away from each other, clearly unnerved and bitter at the idea of being similar—again.

"Yes," Kitty continued, refusing to notice their awkward moment. "I have dreamt of it for years now, but it wasn't until two years ago that I had the courage to attempt it. I realized, over time, that there was nothing to fear."

"Did you tell your sisters of your dream?" Colonel Fitzwilliam asked.

"No," I said, "we were quite in the dark about it."

"I made a habit of saving any scrap of paper in the house and keep from throwing it out," Kitty explained. "For example, when mama wrote down her grocer list, or there were receipts from purchases, or anyone threw away any paper that had nothing written on the back side, I furtively procured it, and used it for my scribblings." She leaned forward, conspiratorially. "And I also learned something important."

"What?" Georgiana asked.

"That the best way to achieve something is to do it completely in secret. If you are smart, never fully let on how smart you are. If you are ambitious, do not make it consistently public. If you are in love, do not immediately declare it. Time always has a way of working much out eventually, and opportunities arise when you least expect it. Of course, eventually, you must act! We all must act eventually. But it is best to do it at the proper moment."

"You were never actually aloof and simple, were you?" I asked. "Kitty, were you secretly complex?"

"I do not know," she confessed. "I believe that I was, but after allowing everyone to think that I was foolish and had a love for soldiers, dancing, and parties, I found that I like the simplicity of having a mind of simple aims. I realized that smart people can sometimes make their minds miserable because they are always thinking of ways to complicate their lives. So, I gave my mindset to my heroines: what path should they choose? To be smart, or to be pleasant? That is one of the many paths that they walk down."

"And what is your book about?" Colonel Fitzwilliam asked.

"I could talk about it all day," Kitty said, "and I wonder now that perhaps I do not have the right. I shall talk about my book another time, but for now, it is Elizabeth and Mr. Darcy's day. So, it should be about them."

"Thank you, Miss Kitty," Mr. Darcy said, "perfectly put, for you show consideration of us."

---

The punch was brought, Colonel Fitzwilliam offered a toast to our good health, and we drank a cup of it merrily. Then tea and cakes were brought in.

Now all seated, Mr. Darcy and I began to tell our story. Yes, we began right at the very beginning!

From the second that Mr. Bingley and his company arrived at the assembly room for the dance, to when Georgiana encouraged me to tell Mr. Darcy how I felt.

This narration first pleased Colonel Fitzwilliam, but then it took a turn where it gave him some pain. After all, Mr. Bingley had been there from the very beginning. Therefore, he could offer little anecdotes here and there, strengthening Jane's memories of him.

Jane was not stone. Naturally, she was affected by all of this, and it showed as she smiled at some moments.

When my narration reached the Netherfield Ball, all of us, except Georgiana and the Colonel, became animated. For it was a memory that we all shared.

"Do you recall, Darcy?" Mr. Bingley brought up, "when Miss Lydia Bennet pressed me to give a ball, and my sisters and you were very much against it, initially. But despite being very occupied with my own happiness at my choice of dance partner," –here he looked at Jane, and she blushed— "I now recall that you and Miss Elizabeth danced together there."

"It was our very first dance," I said. "And I wondered what you had been thinking?"

"That was the very thing," Mr. Darcy admitted. "That was when I first stopped thinking about it. At that point, I had been in love with you."

"That far back?" Mr. Bingley questioned.

"Yes. That far back. But I was against acting on my feelings. As you said, Kitty, discretion is sometimes the better part of survival. But I concealed my affections, all because I was against the idea of falling in love at the time. Perhaps you could even say that I was an enemy of love."

"And why so?" I asked.

"Well, up until that point, the idea of romantic love had only brought me pain. But that is a story for another time. When feeling such immense attachment to you, Miss Elizabeth, it was bringing forth emotions that I was against feeling for so long. But it was too late; I already felt them. So, I could no longer listen to my mind, but rather I listened to my heart. I stopped thinking and asked you to dance."

"But what of when Miss Elizabeth journeyed to Netherfield Park when Miss Bennet was sick?" Mr. Bingley asked. "Did you secretly admire her actions?"

"Yes, I did," Mr. Darcy admitted.

"He had said that your eyes were brightened by the exercise," Mr. Bingley told me. This new bit of information excited me.

"He did?" I asked, looking at Mr. Darcy. "Is this true?"

"Yes," Mr. Darcy confirmed.

"All that time that we spent running from each other."

"It could be construed as a waste of time, but I believe that you and I had no choice."

"Perhaps we did not," I agreed. "My friend, Charlotte Lucas, had a prescription for getting a husband, which was that it is better to know as little as you can about the defects of one's married partner. I could not live under such a prescription. And neither could you. We had to learn of each other's defects and confront them first. Like two stubborn mules."

"The defect you cast at me was the propensity to hate everyone," he noted.

"And the defect you accused me of was the willfulness to misunderstand them. How right and wrong we both were of each other. I suppose that you are right. We had no other way."

"It makes sense," Colonel Fitzwilliam said, "for if true love were easy, we all would have it." And here he looked at Jane, who bit her lip, upset at the pain that both men were feeling.

We continued to narrate our love story. Once we reached the point where Colonel Fitzwilliam entered, the Colonel grew livelier, and was happy to discover just how much we owed our happiness to him. Every now and again, he added a detail that we forgot.

Amid this all, I looked at Mr. Bingley and the Colonel and marveled at the part both men played in our tale. In some way, both brought Mr. Darcy and I together.

Mr. Bingley had come to Hertfordshire, bringing Mr. Darcy with him. He also hosted the ball at Netherfield Park, where Mr. Darcy and I enjoyed our first dance.

Colonel Fitzwilliam was there to explain the truth about Mr. Wickham's real behavior and clear Mr. Darcy's name. This inspired me to seek Mr. Darcy in London and persist in making amends. Both men directly led to my fate. I owed them both.

But rather than it be solely that, fate had repaid them by placing them as rivals for the same woman's hand. This was not fair at all.

And Jane had no choice but to be their emotional battleground. They would never do anything to hurt her, but their current distress was pain enough for her to be a casualty in their fight for love.

Eventually, we finished our tale and an hour had passed. This lengthy story proved proper because we all had something to contribute to the story. Mr. Darcy and my love story were something that they all played a part in, and it could even be said that sometimes a village helps bring about a bond. Who would have known that were possible?

When all was said and done, it had been a long enough visit for both gentlemen. But in case they still wished to carry their point, Mr. Darcy made the visit final in the best way imaginable: indirectly.

"Friend and cousin," Mr. Darcy concluded, "you both have been kind and listened to us all ramble on about something that has caused this happy moment. By listening to us, you have shown that you care for our union, and it means the world to me. I recall that you have something important to say. So… what is this announcement that you need to make on *the most important day of my life*?"

This stressing of his last words made it evident that both men should *not* make any announcement at all, and they took the hint.

"I just wished to tell you that my regiment is staying in London and so you shall have to suffer my company longer," Colonel Fitzwilliam said.

"And that I shall also be in town and will feel very humble if I am allowed to pay visits," Mr. Bingley intoned.

"You are always welcome," Mr. Darcy said.

"Yes," Jane voiced meekly. "We shall look forward to seeing you both."

Both men did not know how to receive such news. She had said it to both and not to one solely. But this was how it should have been.

Both men took their leave and Mr. Darcy escorted them to the door. When doing so, Jane stood up and sighed, somewhat relieved.

"Elizabeth and Miss Darcy, please tell Mr. Darcy that I am

sorry, but I have suddenly gotten a headache and need to retire to my room."

"We understand," Georgiana said.

Jane left the room. Soon, Darcy returned, and we explained where she had gone.

"Miss Kitty," Mr. Darcy said, "can you go and ask your sister if she will want her dinner to be served in her room? I have the suspicion that she might."

"That is a smart thought," Kitty said, standing up. "Yes, I can."

She left and Georgiana sat there, wondering what she should do.

"Miss Georgiana," I said, "I know Kitty, and she will want to speak to you in confidence as soon as she can about her *book*. And she would like to tell you if Jane wishes to eat with us or not."

She understood my meaning, which was my way of saying 'my sister will want to talk about everything that just happened'.

"I would like to hear her words on it," Georgiana said merrily and then she left the room to find Kitty. Now that we were alone, I took Mr. Darcy's hands and kissed his lips.

"Sir, you handled that very well," I complimented him.

"My stubbornness is the real hero here," he said with a smirk. "For while I am willing to suffer awkwardness in other places, I refuse to do it in my own house."

I laughed.

# CHAPTER 2

## SISTERLY ACCEPTANCE

*W*hen we were alone together, in his study, Mr. Darcy and I could not help but sit alongside each other—in truth, I sat on his lap while he placed his hand along my thigh and our heads rested against each other.

"I never knew that you were so skilled in the art of diverting people from their point," I acknowledged. "Remind me to be wary of that if we ever get into a fight."

"You are engaged to a man who admits to liking getting things his own way."

"All humans prefer that."

"Yes, we do. Thank you, Elizabeth. Yet, I cannot attribute my actions today to cleverness. Rather, it was from a place of sensibility. This day was supposed to be our day. It was supposed to be perfect, with us announcing our engagement, and every one of us being happy this day. Yet, both men entered, determined to carry their point, and I was not going to have that. No. I would not let this ruin anything for us."

I looked at him and I beheld the depth of his eyes. Words were not needed. I admired his passion and agreed with it. He was protective of our special moment, shielding it from anything that could raze it. Between us, we understood each other. The longing and expectations of the day had raised our spirits and increased our desires to be together in every fashion. Leaning forward, our faces drew near each other, and we kissed. It was long and our lips lingered, leaving me to be overwhelmed at the beauty of the action.

Eventually, our lips parted, and I opened my eyes to discover a twinkle in his.

"Did I do that well?" I asked.

"Marvelously," he answered. "In a way that I had not experienced it before. Did it feel… organic to you? Natural?"

"Yes, it did."

"That is how it should be. Kissing is not an art that everyone has."

"Does that give me leave to assume that I am perfect for you?" I asked, my eyebrow arching. "If we are unified in that action, and it felt so right, then we are in a proper accord."

A smile escaped him.

"I shall take it as a sign as well."

"And I made you smile. I enjoy it when I do that. But this action is altogether surprising for me."

"How so?"

"Well, I did not expect this. What I mean is that… when you are a young woman, you are constantly told to marry well, and that is your chief duty in life. But compile that lesson with the model of marriage that my parents portrayed, and you must understand that I did not think I could ever fully consider intimacy being something a woman could enjoy. I do not recall if I ever saw my parents kiss."

Mr. Darcy squinted as he looked ahead of me.

"What?" I asked. "A shilling for your thoughts?"

"It is just—now that I think of it, I never saw my parents kiss either."

"You too?"

"Yes."

Considering this, I marveled at the concept.

"Now that we have taken time to expound on the idea, is it not fascinating? Many people do not show affection for their spouse in public, and yet we knew to kiss. I wonder how we even learned of the action when so many people around us do not ever kiss the one they love, in a public setting. In fact, the first moment that I can place on me seeing a husband and wife kiss was when I was a child. It was one of the servants in our house. She was married to one of the farmers that was under my father's employment. Her husband passed away a couple years ago, but they were affectionate with each other. One time, as I was playing with Kitty at Longbourn, I saw them both kissing in the field. That was the first time. And every other time that I saw it, it was also always with another set of people of the lower class."

"I can attest to a similar experience," Mr. Darcy empathized. "The first time I saw such an act of affection was when my father's steward kissed his wife when she came to visit him. The steward doted on his wife terribly, to the point where she spent more money than he earned."

"Are you referring to Mr. Wickham's father?"

"Yes. I refuse to let the actions of the son sully the reputation of the father."

"But it still stands. We both only learned of intimacy due to seeing others display it, and not our parents."

"And those that we did see show their affection for each other were of the lower classes. This perhaps gives the lesson that public displays of affection belong to the poor and not to the wealthy."

"Example would suggest that. It's a wonder how we got on. You and I were perhaps subliminally taught that such displays of passion were not logical. But I liked what we just did."

"I have been longing for such intimacy between us for quite some time."

"And we have been missing so much time by doing anything but," I chuckled.

"We shall make up for time that we wasted, I can assure you," he vowed. "We shall be man and wife soon. And now that I know that your passion is equal to my own, we do not have to be logical. We can express our feelings for each other quite often."

I gave him a warm smile. "I marvel at you. All that grace, elegance, and refinement, and underneath it all… you have it within you to be wanton and passionate. I hope that this irony of nature will always exist in you. I do not want to be like my parents.

I see it now, more than ever. Expressing your feelings through word and action is something that I will always enjoy."

"And I with you. We shall marry soon. I promise."

I rested my head against his. "I would agree with you, but there is one thing that impedes our way."

His eyebrow raised.

"And what would that be?"

"My mother."

His expression changed.

"Oh. Yes! There is the matter of her."

"She will demand that we marry in Hertfordshire, where she will show me off. You know the woman who gave birth to me."

"Yes, I do," he said with a sigh. "She will make our lives difficult if she does not have her own way, won't she?"

"She will be so hard-pressed on having her own way that she will do something that she doesn't often do."

"And what is that?"

"Write me letters about it."

He flinched.

"Somehow, I see the gravity of that situation."

"I suspected that you would. For her character is always less difficult to dissemble."

Mr. Darcy rubbed his eyes, frustrated.

"I wish to marry you tomorrow."

"As do I. But we have other matters to think about."

"Such as?"

"Jane, your friend and your cousin."

"Yes. That beast!"

I kissed him once more and then stood up.

"Where are you going?" he questioned, with a sharpness to his tone. "I thought you enjoyed this moment alone."

"We have had more than a moment," I corrected him teasingly, "and this will be good for us. You and I seem to be of the same mind right now, and we do not desire to ever leave this room. But if we do our duty by being attentive to our family now, then we shall learn how to suffer being social even when we want nothing more than to just be alone together."

He leaned back, looking at me. While his face was stone, his eyes twinkled.

"You miss me already, don't you?"

I laughed.

"All this time, you have left us so much in the dark about your real character! You have the demeanor of a marble statue, but underneath it all, you want to be loved all the time. Do not deny it?"

"For you, and only you, no, I will not deny it."

Smiling, I was suddenly struck with an idea.

"I have a plan."

"You are the sort of woman who schemes?"

"You are surprised?"

He chuckled.

"I will speak with Jane, see if she is amenable to the idea. If she is, then I will tell you about it."

"Or you could tell me now?"

Smiling, I didn't answer his appeal and rushed out of the room. I could only imagine what he was thinking. But it was a thing where you cause pain to cause pleasure later on. Hopefully, he understood that I was merely teasing him.

I rushed up the steps to Jane's room. Reaching the door as soon as Kitty exited it, we both gave each other a look.

"Is she willing to talk to another sister about her predicament?" I asked.

"I believe so," Kitty said, "now I must tell Georgiana everything. It would be ungrateful to keep her in the dark."

"Yes." Struck by an idea, I grabbed Kitty's hand. "Kitty, tell me the truth. This whole day... what are the chances that you are going to use this as inspiration for your writing?"

She rolled her eyes.

"And this is why I didn't tell anyone for so long, besides the fact that I was not very good when I began. I worried that you all would be wondering how much of reality did I draw inspiration from."

"I am not upset with that," I assured her, "because you have already promised to conceal our names. I just wish to know how much, so that I always know to prepare myself."

"Very well. I shall make a bargain with you. I will only tell you if you promise that you will not live your life always fearful of what I write, and therefore distancing yourself from me."

"Don't worry. I have never been afraid of pens or swords my entire life."

"Do I have your word?"

"You do. Nothing will ever stop me from being myself."

"Good. Then I confess all. I will not use *all* of what occurred."

I smirked.

"Mystery solved, and I am satisfied."

"So am I," she said. "I am happy that we have solved that matter. Now, go to Jane."

"And you to Georgiana."

"This is a day of necessary conversation."

We both parted ways.

Knocking on Jane's door, I waited for her reply. In a flash of a moment, I thought of my poor late father and then my mother back on Longbourn. I wondered what they would have thought in that moment, of how it all had turned out.

"Come in," Jane said.

I opened the door and Jane was removing her shoes.

"Jane," I began, "I know that you must be sick of speaking about what just occurred."

"On the contrary," Jane assured me. "I am in want of advice on how to handle myself."

"Really?" I asked. I closed the door behind me, crossed to her bed, and sat down. "You are?"

"Yes. Lizzy, I am not so delicate that I am afraid to confront the situation. Two great men have come here, on your most special day, to…"

"Make you an offer of marriage."

"Yes. I am heartily flattered that both men have held me in such high regard, and to know that our mother has always dreamed of us getting married. But this is not what I wanted. At all."

"I can very well believe it. This must be very hard for you."

"Speak nothing of that. This situation is harder on both men. They must be so miserable. I am so happy that Mr. Darcy organized the conversation to focus on you both. It was how it should have been to begin with. But it also gave me time away from one of the most distressing dilemmas of my life. Funny!"

"What is?"

"Most of the years as we grew, we were so focused on romance, falling in love and getting married. And now the reality has caught up with our minds, and I do not know how to take it all in. I confess that it all seemed so much more organized and enjoyable in my head."

"Of course," I explained, "because in our minds, our fantasies are controlled. They are dreams that we think of, in the day, and since they are dreams that we control, the situation plays out precisely as we wish. That makes it so very much impossible for reality to ever live up to our dreams. It is a path that we all have to walk down and learn to balance."

"I never dreamed of two men falling in love with me at one time, so yes, my dreams did not prepare me for this. I know that I sound ungrateful, but this is not what I wished for at all."

"You are not ungrateful," I assured her, "because now you are put in a place where you must choose one and hurt the other."

"That is the difficult part of it. I do not... no, it is more than that. I CANNOT hurt one of them. The idea of it is too painful for me to bear."

"I suspected that was how you felt," I noted. "But, out of curiosity, is there one that you lean more towards?"

"That is the worst part of the conundrum. Lizzy, is it so strange that my heart is big enough for two of them to be in there at one time?"

"You are in love with both of them?" I asked, surprised.

"I know that sounds unnatural, but you must understand me. My affections are the sort that originate from an amalgamation of many traits that both men have. First, despite my lack of wealth, they found me worth loving. Also, they are both very agreeable, charming while also being sincere, and are the exact sort of men that I have always favored. They possess all the qualities that I admire. And when Mr. Bingley left me behind, my heart then became available to open it up to Colonel Fitzwilliam. I was prepared to fall in love again. Once doing that, it was easy to get on. Only for my first love to fall back into my life after I began to enjoy the second. This is not how it should be. But it is."

"I had a feeling that your heart would be torn in two like this."

"You did?"

"Yes. I was hoping to be wrong, and I am sorry that I was not. But we also must be considerate of the men now. Here is my plan. Hopefully, it will not be injurious to you. But the men have the right to speak their point."

I told her the plan and, despite that she would prefer not to undergo it, she was willing to agree to it. After all, both men had the right for this.

When she agreed, I told her that we had to inform Mr. Darcy.

---

Standing in front of Mr. Darcy's desk in his study, Jane stood by me as I began to explain my plan.

"Jane has agreed with me," I began, "that this is the only course of action."

"Ah," he replied, giving me a wicked look. "Here comes the plan that I am hearing for the first time."

He clearly had been affected by my teasing.

"Despite the pains that such a situation can incite," I continued, "I suggested that we write to Mr. Bingley and the Colonel. We accept their right to each offer their proposal to Jane and she chooses which she prefers."

"Truly?" he said, looking at Jane. "This would make you happy?"

"Their pain brings me no pleasure," Jane said. "But nor does my silence. Sadly, I have accidentally encouraged two men at one time, and that is my fault."

"It is not your fault," Mr. Darcy countered. "It is a mixture of my fault for encouraging Mr. Bingley not to marry anyone when in Hertfordshire, and it is also his fault for considering my advice over the matters of his own heart. I am to blame for interfering, and he is to blame for not strengthening his will against mine. Others are culpable, but not you. And, when considering it, if I had not encouraged Mr. Bingley to ignore his heart and was more sensitive to your feelings, then you would not be in the situation for which you find yourself now. I suppose, in the end, this perhaps is my doing."

Jane gave him a grateful smile.

"You were trying to be considerate of Mr. Bingley, so I will always forgive you for your past interference. I know what you did was in the service of a friend."

"Thank you," Mr. Darcy answered.

"Yet, all that matters now is that we let the gentlemen no longer suffer. I give you permission to write to them both, arrange for them to visit tomorrow at two different times and I shall hear them out. They both deserve that much. And if I result in making one happy, but injuring the other one, then hopefully the latter's pain shall not be long-lasting."

"I suppose that this is the only course of action that can be taken," Mr. Darcy accepted. "I shall write them both an express letter post-haste."

"Thank you."

After that, Jane left us alone.

"And that was the plan that you left before telling me?" Mr. Darcy asked, standing up.

"Yes, it was," I challenged. "Despise me if you dare."

Slowly, he came from around his desk, with a determined look in his eye. For some reason, I understood what he was feeling. So, I proceeded to back away. Somehow, this only excited his desire for pursuit.

"No," I protested.

"Yes," he asserted. Then he rushed after me and chased me around the room. Eventually, he caught me and held me tightly. At last, we collapsed on the divan.

"You dared to tease me," he challenged, his lips pressed against my cheek.

"I dared. And I will dare again."

"You will not ever punish me again."

"I will, once more, as always."

"Kiss me."

Turning my face to him, I narrowed my eyes.

"No."

He pressed his nose against mine.

"Elizabeth…"

Giving in, I kissed him.

# CHAPTER 3

## POSTSCRIPT

*T*he next day arrived, and four letters were received. First, there was one letter from Colonel Fitzwilliam, happy that he was offered a time to carry his point. He said that he would call on us at 3 o'clock. Mr. Bingley said that he would call at 2 in the afternoon. Surely an hour would be enough for them to express themselves.

"Proposals that are timed," Kitty noted. "Never would I have thought that a man would have to schedule an appointment to display his proposal. Well, this is what I call an interesting element of the 19th century."

"I pray that nothing so inorganic ever passes through this house again."

"There is more to Mr. Bingley's letter," Mr. Darcy informed us. "Mr. Bingley says that his sister is back in town and wishes to call on us."

I rolled my eyes.

"Never mind. Something very inorganic *is* going to pass through this house."

The next two letters were from two different sets of relatives. The first was from Mary, who wrote to tell us some unfortunate news. Seeing that it was important for everyone to know, I decided to read it aloud.

Dear Lizzy, Jane, and Kitty,

It has often been said that idle hands led to the devil's mischief, and I believe that truer words have never been spoken! For what do you think has occurred since you are quite gone away?

The regiment is to leave Meryton and are camped at Brighton for the rest of the winter.

Lydia has been invited to go, by Mrs. Forster, as her particular friend. And Mama has agreed!

Lizzy and Jane, I begged her not to allow Lydia permission to go, but I might as well have never spoken. My pleas fell on deaf ears.

While I love our mother, let us be honest with ourselves. Lydia has always had a special spot in her heart, and she has often given Lydia the best treatment... to the point where Mama is guilty of offering an unhealthy amount of indulgence. I tried to tell her that if Lydia were to go, she would be beyond the reach of amendment. She would become the most ridiculous flirt that ever made herself and her family ridiculous.

Kitty, I know that you favor Lydia as well, but please, I would advise you not to follow her example and give way to such outward displays of impertinence.

For mark my words, she will be censored and despised everywhere that she goes. I do not want you to suffer such a fate.

Lydia will go to Brighton, and despite that Mrs. Forster and Colonel Forster will care for her, I still do not believe that they will succeed in controlling her. How do we know that she won't get into some form of mischief now that she has no proper chaperone? There will be officers aplenty and parties almost every night. I feel that she is lost, in the sense that now she will never be encouraged to apply herself to serious application.

I just wish to inform you and keep you abreast of news at home, despite that everything is out of my hands. At this point, Lydia has just left and is on her way to Brighton with the Forsters.

I am heartily upset about all of this. And I wish, now that

father is gone, Mother would apply herself to encourage Lydia to take matters more seriously. But I fear nothing will ever change.

I pray that Lydia shall learn to enhance herself and that she does not expose herself to the world for foolishness.

Yours etc.
Mary

Closing the letter, Kitty scoffed.

"First," she began, "I admit that Lydia perhaps might expose herself to ostentatious behavior while in Brighton, but you know Mary. She thinks that she expresses herself eloquently, but it always comes out in a condescending manner. She does not know how to convince anyone of her point through easy persuasion. You see how she tries to influence me, but she only insults me. She is all vinegar and no honey. She also does not understand how flaws are on different levels. She equates flirting with being one of the seven most fatal sins. When it can be quite the reverse."

"Kitty," I argued, "Mary is... judgmental. But she is accurate that being regarded as the most determined flirt can sully one's reputation and make Lydia the center of ridicule."

Kitty leaned forward.

"And why?" she asked. "Why is a woman evil because she enjoys speaking to men, laughing with them, showing that she enjoys their company? Why does this make a woman evil? Can either of you answer the logic of that? Of the terrible ill in that?"

I blinked and looked at Mr. Darcy. He, Jane, Georgiana, and I looked at each other, wondering what the answer for this was. We all had the same feeling, but we had no answer.

"Or maybe," Kitty furthered, "it is because there is no real evil in the act of flirtation. It is just simply a maxim that is set down, because the world is so afraid of any real emotion, or because society's idea of being sophisticated is to control us all. And from what I recall, the men that I have spoken with have never had any qualms over the matter. Maybe it was because they were kind. Maybe it was because they realized that being judgmental over innocent traits, like flirtation, was trivial and bitter. Or maybe it's because they finally liked that a woman was not afraid to talk to them." Kitty, at last, looked at Mr. Darcy. "Why are you great men so afraid of us women actually being happy to see you?" Then she looked at Jane and Georgiana. "And why are you other women always so quick to judge us women who have never hurt you, hurt anyone, for not living up to an ideal that doesn't exist?"

This sudden speech took us all off guard and we were not prepared for this.

"And why must there be a uniform way of behaving?" Kitty asked. "I am not you, Lizzy, nor am I Jane or you, Miss Darcy. So why must I act like you when I am not you? Why can I not be Kitty?"

"Kitty," I began, "these are home questions, and I do not deny that there is a great deal of sense in what you say. I admit that even my perspectives on the subject of flirtation can perhaps be extreme. As is Mary's."

"And mine," Jane said, "for my refusal to show my affection for Mr. Bingley perhaps did me no favors. I suppose that the situation deserves a more nuanced approach. Displaying one's affections for a man is best to do only after he displays it first."

"But look what happened, Jane. You did not display your feelings for Mr. Bingley at first, and so he left. You showed affection for the Colonel when he came, so he felt pressed to pursue your company. How is something bad if it works? And what if a woman does not desire the man's romantic affections, but only his company? What then? For that is what I did. I just wished to have fun with male company. But I was supposed to be dull and take no pleasure in anything. How is that sophisticated? And why should it be set down that our actions, as women, must be ruled and dictated by the actions of men first? I do not believe that men are the ones who are oppressing us now. Rather, we are oppressing ourselves. For we are the ones who set the social tone. Therefore, we are the ones who oppress ourselves in this case, because we are the ones to attack each other. And then men encouraged this. Is this the world that we should have our daughters brought up in? A world where they are not allowed to speak about anything else that varies from an invisible script. When we do that, we are not real people, but actors playing a part. And all the while, hiding our true nature. If we do that, then we may have never existed to begin with, because we never truly lived."

She threw down her napkin and she covered her mouth. Her declaration had quite silenced us all.

---

Feeling the weight of her outburst, Kitty was exhausted.

"I am unwell," she said at last, "please, I must ask to be excused."

She stood up and went to the door. Before she exited, Mr. Darcy stood up.

"Miss Kitty," he began, "while the best thing for you to do would be to retire to your room, it might make it hard for you to face us again. Perhaps we should talk about what you have said."

She turned back to him.

"I really did mean all the things that I asked," she continued.

"And while I cannot give you any objective answer, you are the first woman to ask me these questions. I should do my best to answer them."

"You will not make me hate myself for asking these things?"

"No, I will not. We are to be brother and sister soon. I would like for you to be comfortable around me."

Kitty accepted this and she sat back down.

"First," Mr. Darcy began, "I am flattered that you felt comfortable enough around me to ask me these questions. I do not deny that I used to hold open and flagrant flirtation as erroneous for women *and men* to do. But then, I did once censor a woman, once upon a time, for not displaying her affections enough when she was in love with a man. You have touched on the double standards of our beliefs, where we will give you solid answers. For where does affection end and flirtation end? I admit that men and women have a right to display a merriment and happiness with each other, because both sexes find the other amusing. I, myself, do enjoy the company of women, which is why I am very happy to have you all here, beside me."

We all blushed, overcome by his confession.

"But," he continued, "I find that it is best to show affection, even flirtation, toward one another when the feeling is very mutual, there is sincerity in the case, and it is quite between yourselves. But when a woman imposes herself, and a man imposes himself, on the public too much, then propriety has given way. Also, flirtation can be seen as an art and allurement. For my own part, I own to not favoring any art that a woman or man uses to lure someone in. It is all false. Also, if a person flirts with every person of the opposite gender, then that can indicate a want of feeling. What I mean is that if a woman or man flirts with everyone, then how can you expect them to be serious about one person in particular? There is innocent charm and harmful charm. As a result, it's hard to tell when a flirt is being one or the other. So, people naturally label women as the latter."

Kitty considered this and let him continue.

"And then there is the weight of the world. There are many in society who are not averse to a woman flirting. There are even parts of our culture that both tolerate and invite such behavior. I suppose that the tendency of flirtation being regarded as evil is something that elite circles censor and despise. So, if you have ever been criticized for flirting, it is because your family do not want you to suffer under other people's negative remarks. They do not want you to get hurt. Families wish to protect each other."

This point surprised all of us. I never would have expected such a revelation.

"Since you are to be my sister, the last thing that I want to see is you to be exposed to the world for lacking propriety. You are right. Your flirtatious nature has never hurt anyone, and therefore you are neither vicious nor mean-spirited. But we do not want the world to hurt you, so we advise you in other directions—to protect you."

"You wish to protect me?" she asked.

"Yes. I wish to protect you all now. Also, many people attribute flirtation with being an act of artifice. They make it appear as if the one is also the other, and when a woman flirts, it is because she is frivolous and incapable of any deep feeling."

"I can assure you," she elaborated, "that we are capable of great feeling. When you insult us, we hurt. When we are forgotten, we feel the pain of it. When we are ignored, we feel the neglect. And when no one wishes to hear us speak, we worry that our voices will die and that no one cares to listen. We are as human as anyone else. I promise."

"It is true that we forget that sometimes," he noted. "But Miss Kitty, I speak this as a friend. I will never deny that it is always good to be inviting and to make yourself agreeable. But I do not want you to follow after your younger sister's behavior. You can enjoy men's company without always running after them. The reason that I say that is because I wish to protect you once more. Flirtation can lead to a woman placing her faith in the wrong man. Like women, not all men are good. Rattles and rakes are real things and being a flirt can push you in that direction. So, there is that as well. There! That is all that I have to say."

"This is a serious conversation," Kitty said, "and I am not used to being the one to start them, therefore thank you for helping me finish it. First, I thank you for wishing to protect me. I am not used to having anyone thinking to do so."

Jane and I looked at each other, quite embarrassed.

"But," Kitty said, "I do not know how to think or feel right now. I see the wisdom of your words and will do everything in my power to try and be more mindful of my behavior. But I shall never do it so much that my own character gets extinguished. I shall still be myself."

"I understand. I know that I must be confusing you now."

"It is a confusing subject, with no clear answer. You are the first person to confront that it is a matter that is not so simple. I thank you for that."

"We shall agree and disagree on this subject in the future. I know it. But I believe that you and I shall overcome it."

She gave him a warm smile. "Yes, we will. Actually, I feel better already."

Mr. Darcy did not smile, but his eyes twinkled.

"As do I, actually. Now, I have to read the other letter that was sent to me."

Mr. Darcy looked at the name on the letter and his expression dropped.

"What is it?" I asked. "You look alarmed."

"I am," Mr. Darcy replied. "It is from a cousin of mine. Miss Elena Darcy."

"Oh, a cousin. Why do you look disturbed by this? Are you not happy?"

"It is not that I am unhappy. It is just a surprise because I have never met her in the course of my life."

"What?" Jane asked, shocked.

"You have a cousin that you've never seen?" I added. "Was she born in another country?"

"No. She was born and raised here in England."

This confounded all of us. How could two wealthy cousins live in the same country and not make each other's acquaintance at all? Unless...

"In truth," Kitty said to Georgiana, "I never knew that you even had cousins on your father's side. Though, perhaps I should have assumed such."

"You had every reason to think that," Georgiana administered, "since our father hardly ever owned to having two younger brothers."

"There was discord between the three brothers," Mr. Darcy added, "and our father never spoke to his two younger siblings for our entire lives. We literally never saw them, except in portraits. The only reason that we know they had children was because our parents sent them presents every now and again. Elena is our Uncle Lionel's daughter. I wonder what she could have to say to us, despite never meeting."

"I met her," Georgiana said.

Mr. Darcy's head tilted.

"You have?"

"Yes," Georgiana said, hesitant, "when I was at Ramsgate, she was visiting at the same time with friends. And when there, we were thrown together every now and again."

"Why did you never tell me?"

"Because I knew how our father felt about that part of the family… and my time in Ramsgate was not the most pleasant thing to talk about."

"Ah, I see."

"But what was your cousin like?" Jane asked. "Was she a lovely woman?"

"Very. We did not spend time talking with each other for very long, but she seemed to be a lively and good-humored woman. She is also quite beautiful. I recall liking her."

Mr. Darcy opened the letter and quickly turned to Georgiana.

"And she did not forget you, Georgiana, for she writes to you."

Mr. Darcy handed Georgiana the letter and she began to read as we ate. As she did so, her expression changed drastically throughout. First, her face was complacent, then it was surprise, then it turned to empathy and at last acceptance.

"What is it?" Mr. Darcy asked her.

"I do not know if it is something that Elena would wish for me to acknowledge to everyone. But she finds herself friendless in the world and is wondering if she can stay with us for a time."

"What?" Mr. Darcy was stunned.

"Perhaps she is wishing to re-establish a connection with you all," Jane offered.

"You think kindly, Jane, but the reality is the reverse," Mr. Darcy countered. "Her father wanted nothing to do with our side of the family. And as she wrote, she is friendless. Friendlessness is usually the result of some sort of crisis… or scandal."

At the word scandal, Georgiana's eyes widened. We were all able to deduce that *that* had to be the problem.

"Georgiana?" Mr. Darcy repeated.

"I do not know if she would wish of me to speak of it to others."

"We are at an obligatory impasse," I considered. "For you naturally do not want to disappoint her, but you also do not wish to make us feel like we are outside your confidence. I can speak for Jane and Kitty—I believe—in saying that whatever is mentioned now, is not something that will ever leave this house."

"Truly," Kitty stressed, "we do know how to keep a secret."

"I believe they do," Mr. Darcy encouraged, "but that is of little concern. If a scandal is involved, then it perhaps is not so secret."

"It is known amongst the family, but not to any others. But you all are family now, so you have a right to know it. Especially if you choose to let her stay with us, brother."

Lifting the letter from her lap, Georgiana read.

Dear Georgiana,

I know that it shall be strange to hear from me. I ought to feel shame for even appealing to anyone, but if you remember anything about me, you know that I have never been ashamed to ask anyone for assistance. The Darcy pride has never been something that I had much of—but quite frankly, I always found our familial pride to be something that I was always flawed at trying to maintain. Now I am suffering by being unable to live up to that example.

I am forsaken, Georgiana, and I do not deny that it is my own fault. With deception being something that I abhor, I will not lie about any of my actions. But rather, they shall be laid bare at your feet.

My life at home has never been one of gaiety or domestic joy. Therefore, I have been driven to always seek comfort elsewhere, most particularly in the company of friends.

I met a man, a soldier, who I fell deeply in love with. We ran away, to elope, but I soon discovered that his actions were mercenary. He loved me for my money. When discovering this, I refused to follow through with the marriage. Yet, due to my living with him for a time, my parents now prefer to avoid scandal above all things.

But now that my eyes have been opened, I do not care what scandal may arise. I will not marry a man whose sole purpose for marrying me was my dowry. When seeing that I was adamant and not giving into their wishes, my parents have discovered that they can't bear the sight of me and that I shall not return home. I remain in Brighton at the Victoria Hotel, still having enough money to support myself.

Yet, I do wish to be amongst family. Recalling when meeting at Ramsgate, you appeared to be an exceptional woman who was capable of great feeling. Is there any chance that you will take pity on your flawed cousin and take me on as a companion to yourself? I am aware that now I must appeal to your brother.

Mr. Fitzwilliam Darcy, greetings! I am Elena, your estranged cousin—yet we are both aware that that is through no fault of my own. Or yours. We were born under two brothers who were desirous to always have us separate. Yes, you have no reason to assist a relative that you have never met before. So, simply and sincerely, I ask for your help.

My situation was entirely my fault, yes, but as you can see, I never lied about it. Because disguise of any sort is my abhorrence. My behavior was the result of actions of affection and passion for someone who I thought loved me.

I do not deny that I set a poor example of our Darcy pride, but something tells me that you are like your sister, and you possess the Darcy loyalty. We are family, nonetheless. Let us not spend our entire lives not knowing each other just because our fathers wished it.

If you can find it in your heart to take pity on me, then you will have saved my life. And you will have saved me from marrying a man who loves me for my purse.

I am staying at the address on the envelope. Please write back to me quickly, whatever your reply be.

Yours etc.
Elena Darcy

Upon hearing this news, Jane covered her mouth.
"The poor woman!"
"Poor in luck with love, yes," Kitty agreed, "but there is something in her tone that indicates that she is a woman who is not allowing herself to give into despair. She sounds resourceful, for coming to you."
"Darcy," I began, "she really does sound like she needs help and

that she is not malicious. She just seems to have made a mistake of judgment. Georgiana, what was she like when you met her?"

"Charming and confident," Georgiana said, "her asking for help is not an indication of a weak person. You are correct. Her willingness to ask for help was not a sign of someone who was frail, but of a robust woman who has a talent at survival. She is also like you, Fitz. She prefers to tell the truth."

"I would never think to run away and elope." His words were terse.

"Others have made that same mistake and should not be punished forever," Georgiana stated, and I understood the implications. She was referring to herself. She and this Elena Darcy had the same history, and naturally she felt like they were kindred spirits. "Fitz, it is not her fault that our fathers kept us apart. But she really does need our help."

"And perhaps this will be a good thing for you all," Jane said. "Perhaps this is a sign of some sort."

"You may think that, Miss Bennet," Mr. Darcy said, "time will tell if you are correct. I need time to think."

"Will you send a letter today?" I acknowledged, "Time may be of the essence with her."

"I shall send it by the second post," he said. "I need more time to think about it."

"It is something that will take some consideration," I noted, trying to sound lighter. "Nothing like heavy news while eating eggs."

Kitty chuckled.

# CHAPTER 4

## PROPOSALS

$\mathcal{A}$fter breakfast, we parted ways. Kitty went off to write the next chapter to her book. Georgiana went to her room to ponder the situation, and Jane also spent time in quiet reflection.

After all, she had to await two proposals of marriage in one day.

Now at liberty to reflect on his dilemma, Mr. Darcy and I went to his study.

"So," I began, "I know that we must talk about your prodigal cousin, but first, can I say how marvelous you were with my sister? I didn't know what to say, but you did. I wish I could give you an award somehow for…"

I trailed off when I saw a gravity in his eyes. Within his silence were words! Words, words, words!

"For so long," I acknowledged, "I noted that you had a satirical eye. Often, I had misinterpreted that look for a look of hatred. I thought you had despised me."

"Did you really?" he asked, his eyes growing darker.

"Yes. And for all that time, I had been in error. Now I see what that look is."

"And," he continued, walking slowly up to me. "How do you interpret it?"

"It is a look of many things: of passion, of admiration, of affection, but most importantly, of love."

"Yes," he said, finally reaching me. Raising his hands to my face, he caressed my cheeks with his hand. "If you wouldn't mind."

"Never would I mind."

"Good."

Swiftly, he closed the space between us, pressed his lips against mine, and we kissed. Falling into his embrace, I rested my hands on his chest as he picked me up and carried me over to the seat. Once we sat down, he placed his hand around my waist, and we continued to display our affection for each other for a few minutes. Once we bestowed our last kiss, I rested my head against his chest while he ran his hands along the curls in my hair.

"This has been and will continue to be a day that gives you many Trojan horses," I noted.

"I will not let them get past the gate," he responded.

"Am I going mad, or did you just add onto one of my nonsensical jokes?"

"What can I say? I saw the sense in it."

"And first, I have to repeat that I was amazed at your talk with Kitty. It was perfect. Tell me, for I am curious."

"What?"

Settling myself comfortably on his lap, I leaned into him.

"What did you feel when she did have her outburst? I could see that you weren't made of such weak stuff that you were alarmed by it. Rather, you met her reaction with calmness."

"Well, if she had done it in public, I would have been affronted and embarrassed. But she spoke about it to us, her family. If you can't ever speak about how you feel when in the presence of your family, then what is the point of them?"

"You once remarked on my sister's lack of propriety—but then, so have I."

"I have commented on it, but I suppose that it is not their fault. I respect your family, Elizabeth, but your mother did encourage them to behave in certain ways."

"Too true. Now that Kitty is away from mother, I feel that she will improve into her own woman. Yet perhaps we both have been too hard on her."

"I see that she is a good sort of girl, who is just not an expert at deception. When seeing her confess to her own nature, and remark on what is the terrible ill in it, it was a woman who, like myself, does not prefer to lie about things. Like me, she perhaps is ill-qualified at recommending herself to strangers. Maybe, in that respect, she and I are similar."

My eyes widened.

"Am I going mad, or did you just find something in common with Kitty?"

"I did. Besides, you have given me a bit of experience at dealing with a woman who raises her voice to me. After you gave me a proper set-down at Hunsford, I've learned to meet confrontation every now and again."

"It is good to every now and again meet someone who forces us to look at life differently," I said. "If not, then we all would be spoiled. You forced me to inspect a different side to myself. I am happy that you were not upset with Kitty, but rather, you gave her advice without hurting her feelings. At Longbourn, her flirtatious manner was often criticized, but never through a concerned and congenial eye. It was slights, just for the sake of slighting someone. You spoke from a proper place of wishing to improve her—or rather, you encouraged her to improve herself. That is as it should be."

"Or maybe I was still being selfish. I was mean in my previous perspective on her, and I wish to apologize for it. After all, she is correct. Being a flirt is a flaw, but it's not a crime. She is not malicious. And perhaps, when slighting her, others of us allow ourselves to become so. What is the point of ridiculing someone if you are guilty of worse?"

"It is not fair for you to be wiser than me in this moment," I teased. "Mark my words, I shall be wiser than you tomorrow. If, at breakfast, the first choice is butter, I shall propose a little bit of jam."

He chuckled.

"Now," I continued, "onwards and upwards, we must speak about the most important thing: your cousin."

"Elena," he said with a sigh.

"So, it really is true that you have never seen her in your entire life?"

"Yes. I know of her, but we never made each other's acquaintance."

"What did it feel like when you heard Georgiana read the letter?"

"Honestly, I felt intruded upon. First, my friend and cousin try to propose to your sister on the day I announce our engagement. Then the next day, we get a letter from our two relatives."

"And both are tragedies that have cast themselves onto Brighton society."

"Yes. This should be our time, but it's not."

"How sad it is that the world never stops for anyone," I said. "And we have to suffer the same fate. Now, it comes down to it. Will you have Miss Elena come to stay with us all?"

"It is very difficult. First, I am having trouble feeling compassion for someone that I never met before. And the scandal of it all."

"And that is the reason why I would recommend us taking your cousin in. Because of the scandal, she has been forsaken. That is a poor lesson to teach the world: let your family fall to ruin just because of one little mistake that has no lasting repercussions. And we must think of Georgiana. Because of her situation, she will always feel that a part of her is separate from the rest of us—a part of her that only a mutuality of action can help. None of us here has almost eloped, but she has. Yet this Elena Darcy clearly has also done so. Therefore, by having her come, Georgiana will feel like she has found a kindred spirit. Also, by seeing you willingly take such a woman into your house, it shall only fortify Georgiana, because it will show how you forgave her, not just because she's your sister, but also because you are tolerant of human frailty."

He looked away from me, out of reflection.

"I had not thought of that," he considered.

"My consideration is recompense; after all, if you were kind to my sister, then I ought to be considerate of yours." He turned to me, his eyes twinkling. "There!" I laughed. "It turns out that I didn't need to wait till breakfast tomorrow to find some way of being clever."

The doorbell rang.

We both checked the clock.

It was Mr. Bingley, who had come to propose.

---

Stories have so many perspectives that they cannot always be seen by all. So, the tale must be directed in a manner, every now and again, away from one point of view and focus on another.

Elizabeth and Mr. Darcy met Mr. Bingley with cheery civility, to display their respect for him, no matter how the situation ended. Yet neither of them was there to see how the proposals occurred.

Therefore, the point of view of the narrative must shift to Miss Jane Bennet, who heard Mr. Bingley's voice from her room. When it was time, Elizabeth walked up the steps and went to Jane.

When seeing her sister there, looking a little wary, Elizabeth was empathic.

"If you like, I can always sit on the other side of the room while the gentlemen make their proposals. I can see that you are a little shaken by the prospect of having to meet with them."

"Thank you, Lizzy," Jane said, "and I do wish for you to not leave me alone. But I will not be selfish now. Both men have come to propose, and I owe them the chance to speak to me, unfettered and not overheard. Besides, if I cannot face a man proposing to me, then I need to be made of stronger stuff."

Elizabeth joined Jane, and they walked down the steps together. When Jane saw Mr. Darcy waiting for them, she breathed a sigh of relief. She worried that Mr. Bingley would be the first face that she met, and it caused her anxiety.

"Miss Bennet," Mr. Darcy explained, "Mr. Bingley is waiting for you in the drawing room."

"Yes," she said, smoothing out her dress. "I fear that no matter what I do, I will not be prepared for this moment."

"I do not think that anyone would be," Elizabeth offered.

"Lizzy and I will be in the sitting room next door," Mr. Darcy stressed. "When you feel as if you wish to end the visit, you may tell him that you wish to have a day to consider his offer, come out of the room and I shall conclude everything."

"Thank you," Jane said, comforted that he and Lizzy would be right in the other room.

Breathing in, Jane walked to the drawing room's door, turned the knob, and entered.

When she stepped in, she saw Mr. Bingley pacing back and forth. When seeing her, he stopped immediately.

"Miss Bennet." Mr. Bingley bowed.

"Mr. Bingley," Jane said, curtsying after she closed the door. "I trust you are well."

"I am," he replied, "and might I say that your beauty is even more evident today. It reminds me of the first day that I met you."

"At the assembly."

"Yes. It is a moment that I think about often."

"Those were simpler times," Jane offered. "So much less cares."

"We had just met, your father was still..."

"Yes."

"You must miss him."

"I do," Jane responded. "Our lives felt like they would have never been the same again."

Jane walked up to the sofa and sat down by the fire.

"Forgive me," Mr. Bingley pointed out, pacing back and forth again. "Here I have come to offer my hand to you, and I only remind you of your tragedy."

"Oh, but I liked that you spoke of it," Jane assured him. "It shows that you care."

Mr. Bingley smiled bashfully.

"Thank you. Miss Bennet—Jane. I am aware that my absence from your life is greatly not in my favor. For one evening, I am showing my blatant preference for your excellent company, and then I leave, without one word about my departure. I know that I have no right to ask for your hand. Yet, I believe that you, who are all goodness and affability, will offer me a chance to explain myself."

Jane folded her hands on her lap.

"I am willing to listen," Jane assented.

"First, I am a man who sometimes is so foolish that I allow myself to be persuaded by others. When friends and family speak to me, I listen. Being victim of over-persuasion has always been my greatest flaw. Truly, sometimes I have leaned on Mr. Darcy's opinion so much, for fear that I might find myself wandering into a duckpond if I do not. Yet, please remember that many of my company advise me out of the goodness of their hearts. I was convinced, by my fragile modesty, that you were indifferent to me. That perhaps, you valued my company, but that you did not reciprocate the same passion that I felt."

Jane raised her eyes at this.

"Indeed, that is what you thought?"

"Yes. Others suggested, due to your lack of outward displays of affection for me, that you did not feel as I did. And I, when reflecting on it, thought perhaps I was projecting my love for you onto you, without noticing how you felt."

"You thought that you saw love in me that was not there?"

"Yes."

Disturbed by this, Jane stood up and walked to the window and gazed out.

Apprehensive about this silence, Mr. Bingley did not move. Yet he only stood there, watching Jane intently. How beautiful she looked! Indeed, she was always beautiful, but now, seeing her there, in disturbed reflection, a fire erupted within him. His passion rose with every moment at the possibility of obtaining her. Naturally, his present ardor was the result of the longing that comes from wanting something that has not been obtained yet. As painful as it is to admit, the longing for something is always more enjoyable than actually obtaining it. This observation is not rational, but nonetheless, it is true. Of course, no one ever thinks about that when they are in love.

Jane was unable to face him, for she felt so overpowered by Bingley's confession.

"Forgive my silence," Jane began.

"There is nothing to forgive," Mr. Bingley rushed out. "I have been the one who was entirely in the wrong."

"It is not your company's fault that they thought that I was indifferent. Sometimes, out of my own natural inclination to not impose myself upon others, my feelings can be repressed. Therefore, I cannot deny that my appearance can be deceptive. I can appear indifferent when I truthfully do feel deeply. And since none of you knew my character, you were left in the dark. This is such a blow to my self-awareness. Recently, I have become aware that my character can be too sedate. So, this is a painful thing to confront."

"There is nothing to confront," he assured her. "Your serenity of countenance is one of the things that drew me toward you. Your goodness, your loveliness, and your genteel nature have nothing to apologize for. Between my own foolishness and my inability to trust my own instincts, I neglected you—exposing myself to the world for caprice, and you to its derision for disappointed hopes. And I involved us both in misery of the acutest kind. I have been in torment since we separated. My mind was never long away from thinking about you. I worried that you had chosen another, and I feared the idea. Every woman I met never made me forget you. Rather, my mind's eye always put your face in her place. I am aware that I come now after you, perhaps…have learned to feel for another. But I feel it still my right to try and win your heart. Miss Jane Bennet, the angel that you are…will you give me the option of offering you my hand, my heart, my life and my wealth? I will spend my life always looking after you, protecting you and loving you. Every day of my life will be directed to giving you the best life that is in my power. And above all, I shall love you."

Jane closed her eyes in pain. His proposal was so lovely and so well put, that it pulled at her heart. A part of her did still love him tremendously, however, the other half of her heart was still tied to another. And she felt her soul crushing even more. But in that moment, a part of her cried out to accept Mr. Bingley's offer.

"Mr. Bingley," she said at last, "I thank you for the offer of your hand in marriage. It was beautiful, truly, it was the most beautiful thing that I have ever heard. Had there been no impediment to my heart, I would have accepted you in this moment."

"No impediment?" he repeated, his voice hollow.

"This is not a rejection," Jane assured him. "This is to explain why I need more time to reflect and decide where my heart lies. I am sensitive to everything that you said, and it has reached my heart. I am sorry that my previous lack of emotional display ever gave you the impression that I was indifferent. And this is the only answer that I can give you: I was never indifferent. I always thought of you. Every day, I hoped that I would see you, for I never met a man who I preferred more. You had no rival in my esteem. You possessed such happy manners and kindness that I never knew anyone better. Yet, you are aware that I have met another gentleman, and it is only right that I consider what he has to say. I owe him that much. I simply need time to sort out where my mind is."

"Of course," Mr. Bingley said. "I can understand your delay." His spirits were raised, and Jane's declaration and kind voice gave him the impression that he would be ultimately successful. Of course, Jane had never meant anything else but that she *would* consider his offer, but she still had enough presence of mind to be willing to listen to Colonel Fitzwilliam as well.

---

Mr. Bingley did not remain long after his proposal. As soon as he was done, Jane excused herself and went to her room. Mr. Darcy came in, smoothed over the conclusion, and eventually Mr. Bingley departed.

Not wishing to speak about the first proposal just yet, Jane retired to her own reflections until the bell rang again, and Colonel Fitzwilliam had arrived.

The same routine was done, where Mr. Darcy informed him to wait for Miss Bennet in the drawing room while Elizabeth retrieved Jane.

For a second time, Jane and Elizabeth were walking down the steps, to deliver Miss Bennet to a second proposal.

"Is it me, or does it feel like I'm delivering you to a prison sentence?" Elizabeth asked.

Jane chuckled nervously as they reached the door.

"Remember," Elizabeth reminded her, "we are just in the next room."

Once more, Jane turned the knob and entered.

Whereas Mr. Bingley was pacing back and forth, Colonel Fitzwilliam was leaning over the fireplace. Having come from his duties, he was wearing his regimentals uniform and his gestures were smoother in how he stood there. Jane immediately saw how this simple gesture displayed the difference between both men.

Both men were active. Yet Mr. Bingley's lively nature displayed a man who was often on the move, shifting from one place to another, while seeking solid ground the whole time. His comfort was the loyalty to people who were around him. He needed a stable partner, who he could rely on.

Colonel Fitzwilliam, on the other hand, was lively in nature, but there was a grace and elegance to his movements. He was a man who was more rooted to the ground and reliant on his own nature. Yet Jane supposed that it made sense. For Mr. Bingley inherited his fortune, while Colonel Fitzwilliam had to work for his livelihood. Therefore, he had to learn solidarity.

Yet, his handsomeness being augmented by his redcoat, only reminded Jane about how he may have been right for her, but she was not right for him. She brought nothing to the marriage, and he needed everything.

"Miss Bennet," he said, turning to her slowly and bowing. "I know that I must cause you pain in my coming."

Jane closed the door and curtsied.

"How could you think so?"

"Because I am a man who knows the intimidation that love can cause when it becomes quite crossed. Before I begin, Miss Bennet, please give me one more moment to apologize… and you may laugh at me all that you wish in the process."

Jane smiled.

"I would never laugh at your pain."

"Perhaps it might do you good, for I might sound like a fool in the process. I am sorry that Mr. Bingley and I, in our desire to achieve what our heart wants, have put you in a difficult place. Yet, if I were less selfish now, then I would never have the courage to believe that I have a chance. However, I daresay that my nerve, my daring, is what endears us to each other to begin with. For, in every other way, Mr. Bingley is my superior."

"You both have excellent qualities," Jane assured him. "And they are perfectly acquired from each. Neither one of you is superior to the other."

"But he is superior to me in two respects. First, his wealth is something that will lend sparkle to him, where my lack of wealth will have me appear as lead. But also, he had the good fortune to have met you first. Any longer acquaintance with you is a blessing —a blessing that fate and fortune gave him and not me."

He walked up to her, and he reached out his hand. Unable to resist him, Jane took it. Immediately feeling the warmth of it, she was drawn to their connection. He led her to the sofa, and they sat down by the fire.

"You are trembling," Colonel Fitzwilliam noted.

"I confess that I am," Jane admitted.

"I cannot be blind to the fact that it is that situation that causes you to be so."

"Yes. I confess that I am so overpowered now. I am sorry that my courage is not rising to the attempt of it. I am shaking under the weight of affection."

"Would that I could help you," he sighed, his voice deep and his tone passionate. "Would that I could make certain that you never tremble again."

Still holding Jane's hand, he began his appeal.

"Miss Bennet, I have no wealth to speak of. Our lives will consist of me working to support us, and you having to constantly economize to help our happiness thrive. For so long, due to being a younger son, I learned that I was unable to marry where I wished. This has led to me living a half-life. A cursed-life. For I have lost the possibility of women who I felt a deep affection for, and for the fact that I could not support her to bring comfort to our home. Also, I am in a profession where I can experience danger. I bring you little. But I bring you heart. The heart! The thing that I felt stir at the sight of you. For when seeing you for the first time, I felt a change in me."

Jane breathed in heavily, her heart beating strongly within.

"I felt as if all the wealth in the world did not matter. All that mattered was if I had you. I will fight to support us, to give you the life that you deserve. But here and now, I give you my heart, my respect, my adoration. Marry me, my lovely friend. Marry me."

---

When he finished, Jane was so overwhelmed that she almost spasmed as her body was overcome with a spurt of emotional pain. Standing up quickly, she clutched her stomach and moved away from him.

"Have I upset you?" he asked, standing up as well.

"No, you have not," Jane assured him. "You are not to blame. It is just that my heart is affected." Turning back to him, her eyes were filled with emotion. "Why did you have to be so perfect? Why did you have to be so good? If you were not, this would be so much easier. So much better, and I could have made a choice. But no. All your words were perfect. I know that you mean what you say, and that you are a man of your word. I do not deny that I feel a deep attachment to you, and that I enjoy being in your presence. I feel a longing affection that makes me never want to hurt you."

Like it was with Mr. Bingley, she told him that she needed time to form her answer. Then she left the room quickly and Darcy and the Colonel had a few words before the Colonel departed.

And the day of the two proposals had ended.

# CHAPTER 5

## PLANS PUT INTO ACTION

*W*ell, the most dramatic aspects of the day had ended, leaving Darcy and I the ability to exhale. Telling Mr. Darcy that I wished to speak to Jane, we parted, and I went to her room. Soon after I reached Jane's door, I felt the loss of Mr. Darcy already.

That was the painful trick of love!

When you first meet them, you become so dependent on their company that you lose your own sense of inner autonomy. Yet I suppose that to gain something, another thing must be compromised.

Knocking on the door, I asked to come in. When I did, I was met not only with Jane, but Kitty and Georgiana were there. And Kitty had ink on her hands.

"Clearly I was not the only one with the same thought," I observed.

"How can we think of anything else?" Kitty said. "It would be even more improper not to be curious about what happens. Georgiana, is there any chance that you agree with me?"

"I cannot help but be concerned," Georgiana admitted. "After all, one of the men who proposed is my cousin and is also one of my guardians."

"I forgot that the Colonel is your guardian as well, sometimes," I intoned.

We all turned to Jane.

"I came here assuming that you wished to speak about what happened. But if you do not wish to talk about it, then say the word and we will leave immediately."

"I do not mind unfolding my mind to you all, for I am not ashamed of it." Jane sighed as she sat on her bed, pulling away at the tassels on a shawl. "For I have quite made up my mind on the matter."

Kitty, Jane and I looked in between each other.

"You have?" Georgiana asked.

"Yes, I have."

"That was quicker than I suspected," Kitty acknowledged. "I know that you were partial to both men."

"And I am still," Jane augmented, "which is why it has made me find the answer easy."

She paused at this and we all were left in suspense.

At last, she turned to us.

"My mind is quite made up. I shall accept neither of them."

---

Each of our reactions was separate, but equal. Georgiana's jaw dropped open. Kitty sat down in a chair, surprised. And I merely raised an eyebrow.

"Neither of them?" Kitty gasped, "Truly?"

"Yes," Jane persisted.

"But why?"

"Because it is the only way," I spoke for Jane. "The only way to injure neither man more nor less than the other."

"Precisely," Jane elaborated. "They are two worthy men, who are worthy for different reasons. Both of them loved me, but they offered me two different sides of myself. Mr. Bingley stirred my heart in Hertfordshire, but Colonel Fitzwilliam helped me believe in love again here in London. Both have a claim, and both are within my affections. Some may regard me as vulgar for being so plural in my mindset, but I will not repent."

"Well," Kitty offered, "there has never been a rule set down that love must always be similar."

"Perhaps, in some cases, it is best if it were not so," Georgiana added, "or no one would attempt to fall in love again after the first love was lost."

"Yes." Kitty smiled, then she had a thought. "I believe that I shall write our last two sentences down. It will make a good point." Then she turned to Jane again.

"Jane, are you certain that this is where your heart lies?"

"Even if it wasn't, I would still follow this course of action," Jane answered. "For both men do not deserve to feel as if they are lesser than the other. I would never forgive myself if I let one of them think so. I could never be happy that way. Therefore, I shall accept neither. That is the only way that I can spare them the ultimate pain of being slighted."

"I cannot deny that I am happy that you have resolved on that," Georgiana admitted. "I am heartily sorry for the Colonel and Mr. Bingley, but I wouldn't want to see either of them feel as if they did not deserve to be chosen."

"Yes," I assured her, "this is the best thing in the world. They will be upset, naturally, but their vexation shall not be as long-lasting this way. Your conscience is not only clear, but better than ever. I am sorry that you had to resort to this, though. I did want you to find joy."

"I am happy," Jane confessed. "You are to be married, and the burden of having to save the family is lifted from my shoulders. Therefore, I have all the time in the world to find my fate when it finds me."

Jane turned to Kitty.

"More ink on the hands?" Jane asked.

"I cannot help it," Kitty answered. "My thoughts flow rapidly and I do not pay attention sometimes."

"How is your writing?" I asked.

"I am on Chapter 8," Kitty said with a wry smile, "and that is where the real trouble begins for the sisters."

"Well, a little bit of real trouble is always acceptable in a book,"

I said, "and a story without some sort of crisis is too peaceful to be interesting. Kitty, I am proud of you."

Kitty gave me a shy smile. Then I turned to Jane.

"And I am proud of you as well."

I stood up, tapped Georgiana on the shoulder and then went to the door.

"Jane," I finalized, "if you would like, and since it would be most proper, I can tell Mr. Darcy your sentiments and he will write the letter for you. After all, it will be too difficult for both men to want to hear this news in person, and it is improper for women to send letters. I always hated that rule! Either way, by Mr. Darcy writing to them both and telling them what you have decided, that will give them the chance to receive the news in the privacy of their own homes. Under such circumstances, sometimes a person needs to be alone when they hear such news."

"True," Jane said. "If it will not be too much trouble to Mr. Darcy, then yes. Or I can write the letters and he can include it in one of his."

"Never fear," I assured her, "leave it to me. With any hope, you will not have to worry over this for the present… and hopefully for the future."

Kissing her on the head, I left the lot of them alone, overhearing Kitty asking Georgiana if she would read her first chapter of her book.

Going downstairs, I went to Mr. Darcy's study, but he wasn't there. When I asked a servant where he was, I was told that he was in the billiard's room.

Going there, I saw that he was shooting the balls into the pockets. Seeing him there, with his jacket removed and his shirtsleeves rolled up, I noted the physical beauty that he possessed. He cut such a striking figure, with his dark curls resting behind his ears, the sharp elegance of his cheeks and his handsome form. Now, looking on him, I wondered how I withstood his charms before.

When seeing me standing there, he looked up at me and lowered the billiards stick.

"How is she?" he asked.

"Decided."

I told him everything that Jane had said. When done, he complimented my sister on her empathetic nature.

"I profess that I am heartily ashamed of myself for ever thinking lesser of your sister," he informed me, "and I am sorry. Miss Bennet really is a remarkable woman."

"Yes, she is the best creature in the world."

"Second best," he complimented me.

"Or third," I complimented him in turn. His eyes turned dark once more, and I felt the depths of his soul in them. "My sister is perfect in every way, but you... how did I not see your beauty before?"

"Because I made it impossible for you to see it," he replied. "I was blind about things for too long before."

I shook my head and grinned. "How does it feel to wake up to this reality? I bring you dramatic activity and a family whose lives are always on the move."

"I have been sitting still too long, anyway."

"It is improper for you to be so charming now, because it disarms me. I must insult you in some way soon, or I shall go mad by saying too many nice things without one cynical word to break up the monotony."

He raised an eyebrow. "I am not overpowered by being praised."

"Yes, but my wit shall not stay sharp if I do not keep it in practice."

Walking up to him, I pressed my hand against his chest as he wrapped his arms around me.

"Never fear," I said. "I will never give you real trouble. Only enough to present an image of innocent teasing, which will force you to never stop loving me. There, is that suitable?"

"Perfectly so," he said. "Now tell me that you love me?"

"Do you doubt me, sir?"

"Never. Just tell me."

"And this is how I tease you. I refuse to tell you! There, now I have won."

"You have won nothing," he challenged, his expression amused as he leaned into me again. Pressing his lips against mine, he used his passion to disarm me. "Tell me you love me."

"You are not playing fair," I sighed, giving way. "You are using my Achilles's heel against me. You know that I cannot deny you anything when you are like this."

"Yes, I do."

We kissed again. He picked me up and twirled me around. When he lowered me down, I looked into his eyes.

"You were too cruel for hiding how good of a man that you truly are for so long," I said, "now that was true unfairness."

"Call it the last great deception that I will ever do."

Now that it was all resolved, Mr. Darcy took my hand and led me to the door.

"Now, the letters must be written," he said.

"A man's library has often been regarded as his sanctum sanctorum," I noted, "and that is the one place that he wishes to never be met with folly. But we are not married yet, so right now, I will intrude on your space once more again. Yet, when married, I shall let that be your lair of solitude."

"I would like if you remained with me," he said, "for this letter shall be slow at writing."

"And that's where I wish to assist you. I can write the letters to your friend and cousin. Then you can read it, see if I wrote in an acceptable way, and sign your name at the bottom. Women may not send men letters, yes, but if it is only a woman writing a letter for a gentleman, it is still his intent. There! What do you think?"

"I am not averse to it," he said, running his finger along the base of my cheek.

"I thought it would be best since you have another letter to write."

"Do I?"

"Well, you will if you agree to my plan."

"You have a plan? Good god, what sort of woman did I fall in love with?"

"You knew very well the woman that you did. I forbid you to lose your love for me now."

He sat on the billiard's table, and I sat next to him. Unable to resist, he ran the edge of his fingers along the cloth of my gown, along my thighs. I could not feel his fingers through the fabric, but the image of him doing so sent my heart racing.

"I do not enjoy how much my happiness depends on you being near me," I admitted. "I do not like it when you are too far away."

"As if the bond between us will break if we go too far from each other, it will hurt?"

"Yes, that is how it feels. You understand the words are within my very soul. But you speak it first. When I say plan, I do not think of this without considering hearing how you feel about it. I wish us to be agreed on things. So, I ask you to hear me out and consider. For while I do not want you to say no just on impulse, nor do I want you to say yes because you wish to agree with me on impulse. Either one is willful blindness. Can I offer my suggestion?"

"Very well."

"Well, I have a sister in Brighton—a sister who you are aware is not the most rational of creatures. I love Lydia, for she is my sister, but in the heat of the moment, she is not level-headed. Nor can she be trusted. And then there is you, the cousin of a woman who also is staying in Brighton. Perhaps it would be better if, instead of her coming up here, we can go down there and retrieve her. Also, we could stay in Brighton for a time, to see to Lydia. I cannot attest to it, but I have a strange feeling. A bad feeling. I feel as if, if we do not go, something bad will happen. To either woman."

"I am not against the idea, actually. Would you believe, despite all my experiences in the world, I have never been to Brighton."

"I have not either, but you?" I marveled at this revelation. "Well, this is news indeed. Standing up, I faced him. "You, Mr. Darcy, of Pemberley, Derbyshire. An experienced man of information, who has gone out to the world, and yet he has never tasted the delights of Brighton."

"I have tasted better things," he professed, his eyes firmly faced on me.

"Then I wonder, if you agree with the subject you speak of? It is just... you have had to save your sister from a most imprudent elopement. Now your cousin needs your help from recovering from a ruined elopement. And I don't want you to suffer any scandal from anything that my family is capable of. I want to protect you now… and this is the only way that I can think of doing so."

Deliberately, he grabbed my gown and pulled me toward him. When he did so, I placed my hands on his shoulders, and once more, I felt my reserve slip away.

He pressed his face against my chest and ran his lips along my neck as I rested my face in his hair. The warmth of his cheeks against my skin was intoxicating. First, we remained that way, but the sensations of intimacy perhaps gave him courage. I began to tremble under such attentions, for the feel of his lips along the soft parts of my throat, I weakened. Before I knew it, he lowered his lips down to the lace along the top of my gown and he tugged at it with his teeth, pulling it down until I felt his lips begin to move along my breasts.

I was overcome with joy—until I recalled that we were not married. Again.

With all the self-command that I had, I jumped back.

"Lizzy…" he began.

"I… I…"

"Are you angry at what I have just done?"

"No, not at all. I like it when you do such things. But I realize that I am too much willing to give way to you, despite that we are not married. We've already had some incidents, and we should not add to them. You have a way of making me forget myself. I have to therefore try and find my self-control and let it reign over me."

He rubbed his mouth with his hand and turned away from me.

"Please, do not be angry with me," I begged him. "I still feel a longing for you. There! Is that sufficient to help you keep your confidence?"

"I know that you love me, Elizabeth. As I love you. But I am the sort of man who, when he wants something, it eats away at him." Turning back to me, the brilliancy of his gaze was fixed and poignant. "And I have chosen you, so I want you all the time. Add to that the many months that I longed for your company as my wife when we were in Hertfordshire, and my passion has only increased. I will try again, and you have to do your best to withstand me."

Oh, how I loved this man!

"It is a challenge that I welcome. For I am not afraid of you."

I took some paper from his desk, a quill, and sat at a table by the window.

"I will have Kitty write the letter to Longbourn to tell mama and Mary that we will go to Brighton to look after Lydia. She will also tell them the address so that all letters can be forwarded there."

"And I have a letter to write to my cousin, Elena Darcy. The cousin that I do not know."

We both sat down and began our letters separately.

I finished the first letter to Colonel Fitzwilliam and then I began writing the second to Mr. Bingley. While doing so, I could not help but look at Mr. Darcy. Therefore, over my shoulder, I spied him, and I should not have been surprised to see him lower his letter and look at me.

How could I look away? Indeed, every feeling within me forbid me to ignore such a look of pure longing.

Taking my expression for encouragement, he rushed out of his seat, walked up to me, leaned down, and kissed me as he drove his hand into the top of my gown. Reaching under my dress, chemise and corset, he wrapped his hand around my breast and began to stroke it back and forth.

I was utterly lost and could not breathe. Dropping my quill, I felt that I had lost entirely. My resolve had faded, my strength was gone, and I only cared about giving him immediate satisfaction. Raising my hand to the bustline of my gown, I pulled down the top of it so that he could move his hand more easily. Seeing me willing, he shoved his hand more deeply within and moved it over my breasts repeatedly, deepening his touch with each stroke. His kiss was deeper than before, and I gave way entirely.

We were taken aback by a resounding knock at the door and I was so happy for it. Making myself decent, I finished writing as Darcy said the person could enter.

It was his valet, with an invitation from Rosings Park.

Mr. Darcy thanked him and then dismissed him. Thankfully, I was finished.

I placed the letters on his desk.

"There," I announced. "I have finished, and you can read them to see if they meet your standards."

"For a moment," he professed. "I won."

"And here is how you lose afterwards."

I walked to the door, but he grabbed my hand.

"You cannot leave," he urged.

"You have work to do, and I have a fiancé that I have to learn to say no to. We both have our labor cut out for us today."

With that, I left him. And we both were in pain for it.

# CHAPTER 6

## BRIGHTON! ARE YOU FACT OR FICTION?

$\mathcal{M}$r. Darcy had sent the letters to the Colonel and Mr. Bingley, only to send another one soon after, telling them that they would be unable to call, because we were traveling to Brighton.

Letters were also sent out to Mr. Darcy's family members, to inform them that he and I were engaged.

Kitty's letter was written to Longbourn, informing mama and Mary that we were going to Brighton, to join Lydia, and that Mr. Darcy and I were now on the road to marital bliss.

Although, quite frankly, I could not deny that it would be quite the bumpy road on the way to the wedding. For Mr. Darcy and I were not to be trusted and the sensuality that was growing between us was reaching such a pitch, that very soon we might proceed to kick and push each other out of the window at the slightest provocation.

Our marriage would and could result in being... interesting. And I was curious to see how we would endure it. After all, marriages that were entered without affection on either side often followed a pattern of how they ended. But marriages founded on actual love—well, those never followed a definite script.

The Colonel and Mr. Bingley wrote back their well-wishes on us having a safe journey there, and that they understood the decision that was reached in pertaining to them.

"I hope they do not view this holiday as me trying to run away, and you indulging me," Jane said.

"If they do, that is their choice," I assured her. "People think as they wish, no matter what our intentions are. We wish that we could give them peace of mind, but that is only something that they can give themselves."

"Going to Brighton while winter is still fresh is not something they should regard as a holiday," Mr. Darcy clarified, "but in case they misconstrue our adventure, I also mentioned the reasons for our going in my letters to them. They know that we leave for familial reasons and not for escapism. I told them that you all were concerned for Lydia and that I have to retrieve Elena."

"Then there is nothing to fear," Kitty said as Mr. Darcy helped her into the carriage. "Mr. Darcy, I do hope that your cousin likes me."

"If she doesn't, that is her affair," Mr. Darcy said as he helped Jane into the carriage. "And you need not feel any vexation about it. I will make certain that she doesn't look down on any of you."

Kitty smiled, then she turned to Georgiana, who sat next to her.

"What is Miss Elena Darcy like? For if I know what her character is like, then I might succeed at making myself agreeable."

"It has been some time since I have seen her," Georgiana explained, "so her character could be different now. But of what I do remember is that she was not snobbish or quick to jump to prejudice. She also seemed tolerant of people's different and individual character traits. If she is still the same, then I think your natural character is precisely fine."

"Do not be quick to change your whole character just yet," I advised, "for where we are going, it will not ever be needed."

"I believe that Miss Elena Darcy will like us, if we make ourselves agreeable," Jane said as Mr. Darcy got into the carriage and sat next to me.

"That shall be easy," he assured us, "for you are four of the most agreeable women in the country."

We all were elated at his praise.

"Mr. Darcy praises us at the beginning of the journey." I

smiled, taking his hand and kissing it. "Now all that I have to do is make sure that you have a reason to compliment us at the end of it."

He chuckled.

"Only Lizzy can make you laugh," Kitty noted. "Lizzy, how do you do it?"

"By not even trying. I know it is not a logical answer, but it still is the truth."

Mr. Darcy informed the coach to proceed, and with all our luggage safely stored in the back of it, we were off to Brighton.

---

Mr. Darcy and I were in a strange sort of silent agreement. When our sisters were awake, we were willing to fall asleep. When they were asleep, we made sure to be awake. And this was the perfect sort of arrangement. With them still being present, we could not get into any sort of mischief. But with them asleep, we could whisper the romantic nothings that people are oft to do when they feel affection. We could kiss one another and go no further.

After a few hours, we arrived in Brighton by nightfall.

"I am surprised at you," I said to Kitty, as our carriage stopped in front of the Grand Brighton Hotel.

"Why?" Kitty asked.

"Well, I know how much you favored seeing the officers, so when Mrs. Forster's invitation was given to Lydia, I was surprised when you did not care at all."

"I did enjoy the officers, and I still do. I like their company, for they made life interesting. But it also was because they paid attention to me. You cannot deny that people often didn't pay attention to me when I was at Longbourn. But now, you all notice me well enough, therefore, I am less starved for attention."

Now that we were away from home, Kitty's blatant confessions to things no longer appeared irksome, but merely organic. I will say this for Kitty: she always gave a person something to react to.

"I marvel at your ability to speak as you feel without fear," Georgiana said.

"I never learned how to achieve discretion," Kitty admitted. "It was a lesson that there seemed no way of learning when at home."

Mr. Darcy chuckled as he helped Kitty out of the carriage.

"I can very well see how that lesson was skipped. Kitty, I think you will like Brighton."

"I believe that it might be large enough for our personalities," I added.

"And for our desire to start anew," Jane added.

When Georgiana was helped down, we all turned and stood right in front of the Great Brighton Hotel, marveling at it.

"It's beautiful," Jane remarked. "Isn't it?"

"Yes, I believe that it is," I said. "Mr. Darcy, you come with four women wrapped around your arm. And you might have two more on your hands. Your courage shall be tested."

His eyes held a wickedness in them.

"My courage rises with every attempt to intimidate me."

He had echoed my words from when we were at Rosings Park.

"I see you and mark you."

Kitty ran around the carriage and looked out at the view of Brighton from the steps of the hotel. Indeed, it was an impressive town to behold, with the seaside ahead of us in the distance, complimenting the scene of the bathing place that abutted it.

"Brighton!" Kitty professed. "Are you fact, or are you fiction?"

"Fact," came a voice ahead of us. We turned and a lovely woman with dark brown hair was standing in front of the hotel's doors. She was well-dressed and had the air of a lady. "And it's a fact that's even better than the fiction that speaks about it."

"Elena!" Georgiana asserted.

"I was waiting for you at the hotel's front windows," she said, "and you arrived precisely when you said that you would."

We now were facing Miss Elena Darcy. When seeing her, I could not understand the officer who married her for her wealth. Physically, she seemed to be the sort who could win a man's heart simply by her physical features.

"Then you are Miss Elena Darcy?" Kitty said, coming next to Georgiana.

"And you have me at a disadvantage," Elena said, "for I do not know your name. Miss Georgiana, you must introduce me to your friend. For I do not wish to be left in the buff for very long and she seems like the sort of woman that I would like to know."

Kitty blushed.

"In fact," Elena said, looking at all of us, "you bring a whole company to save me. And I like a crowd of this size."

"Miss Elena," Georgiana said, "I bring three sisters, my brother and myself. This is Miss Jane Bennet, Miss Elizabeth Bennet and Miss Kitty Bennet here. And this is the man who I hope that you will love as much as I do. This is my brother, Mr. Fitzwilliam Darcy."

Elena turned to Mr. Darcy.

"So, you are my cousin?" she asked.

"Yes, I am," Mr. Darcy said, bowing. "All our lives we have been separate and yet we are family all the same."

"Thank you both for coming to help me," she said, her tone sincere. Whatever her history, I somehow felt compelled to like her.

"Samuel," Mr. Darcy called his valet. Samuel, who had been riding in the back of our carriage the entire time, came down and stood by his master. "Make all the preparations."

"Right away, sir," Samuel responded. With alacrity, he went inside and soon, hotel workers exited, took our luggage, and greeted us very kindly.

"Forgive me as I marvel at everything," I said to Miss Elena. "Very few moments in life please the eye as this."

"You have not been to Brighton before?" she asked.

"The one negative aspect of country life," I elaborated, "is not to be a creature of the world, but only the creature of a province. Can you forgive a provincial girl and her provincial eye?"

"I can, because something tells me that you have forgiven me for larger things."

The assistants carried our things to three hotel rooms. Mr. Darcy stayed in one, Jane and I were to be placed in another and Georgiana and Kitty remained in the third.

"I shall arrange for us to have dinner in my room, for it has a dining area within it," Mr. Darcy informed us all. Then he turned to Miss Elena. "Would you be willing to attend as well so that we can become better acquainted with you and explain our situation?"

"I would be delighted," Miss Elena said. "Now I shall have to dress for dinner." At first, she began to leave, but then she turned back to us all. "Seeing you all makes me feel better already. For now, I no longer feel alone."

Then she left, going to her room. Before we all went to our separate rooms, Kitty said, "I like her because she makes me feel as if there is nothing to be afraid of."

"If you do not stop successfully keep speaking your mind, Kitty," I said, "I may grow jealous of you."

"It turns out that the best thing I could have done was tell you all that I am a writer. Now you all seem to be prepared for anything to come out of my mouth."

Taking Georgiana's hand, Kitty pulled her into their room. The last thing that I heard was Kitty saying, "You must tell me about every conversation that you had with Miss Elena."

When they closed the door behind them, Jane, Darcy and I were left alone.

"Well, we should dress for dinner," Jane offered, going to our room. Then she gave us a knowing look.

"Lizzy, perhaps I should go in and make sure that our room is suitable and without spiders. I know you fear those. I shall take two minutes to do so. But... no *more* than two minutes."

"Thank you for wishing to protect me from my phobia," I responded. Jane went into the room and left us alone.

Turning to Mr. Darcy, I grinned.

"She does not trust us."

"No, she does not."

"A part of me thinks 'how dare she', and the other half is rational. For I would not trust us either."

"You have a rash and rational side."

"Always, and they conflict with each other. My mind is in a constant battlefield."

Leaning toward me, our faces almost touched.

"Which one will win in this moment?"

"The rash, but I will make sure to listen to the rational after half a minute."

Raising myself up to him, we kissed passionately. After we separated, I looked into his eyes.

"So, we have met your cousin."

"No talk of that now," he said, taking my hand and pulling me to his room. "I wish to talk of other things."

"You do not wish to talk."

"No, I do not," he said with a wicked grin.

"And my rational side is beginning to wake up right now."

I pulled away from him, trying make him loosen his grip on me. Laughing, we fell into a slight encounter of tug-of-war as he tried to pull me into his room, and I tried to pull myself away from him.

Suddenly, we were interrupted when my room's door opened, and Jane emerged from it.

"All is well," she said. "There are no spiders."

"That was two minutes?" Mr. Darcy and I said in unison. Our simultaneous speech shocked us both and Darcy and I were aghast.

Leaning into him, I could not resist.

"We must endeavor to not speak simultaneously again," I teased. "Or I fear that we shall be mocked. That was amusing, though."

"Very amusing."

"Elizabeth?" Jane said. "Your gown will be creased from constantly sitting in the carriage."

"Yes." I gave in, walking away from Mr. Darcy and to our room. Jane gave him a stoic look and then she closed the door behind us.

Now that Jane and I were in our room, I had the suspicion that she was about to speak about my behavior.

"Elizabeth," Jane began.

"I know, I know," I acknowledged as she undid the ties on my bonnet ribbons.

"Do you?" she asked. "I know that you and Mr. Darcy are engaged, but that does not mean that you allow him such liberties."

"I know you are right, but for some reason, whenever I am

with him, my self-command seems to give way and chaos fills my veins."

"Of course, it does, because you are in love," she said as I undid her bonnet's ribbons. "And love is the greatest weapon at dislodging control. I know better than anyone. However, due to Miss Elena Darcy's situation, the last thing that she needs is for you and Mr. Darcy to give into your passions. Naturally, I am aware that my advice will be hard to administer, due to the fact that you are marrying a hypnotic man."

Having begun to remove my shoes, I stopped my activity when she said this.

"You noticed that about him?" I asked.

"Oh yes. Even when you hated him, you could not help but wonder about him all the time. If he did not possess some strange sort of ability, then you would have never mentioned his name again after he slighted you at the assembly. Instead, you focused on him. The more his gaze focused on you, the grander your fascination with him became. Because, even when you despised him, he drew your curiosity."

She sat down and began to remove her shoes and stockings as well.

"What is that like, by the way?" she asked. "To be in love with a man who has the ability to disorientate you?"

"You were in love with Mr. Bingley and the Colonel. Didn't it feel the same?"

"Their love steadied me. Mr. Darcy's love makes you weak in the knees and makes your will blend into his. We are two different sorts of women and he is a different sort of man than them. So, what does it feel like?"

"Like drowning," I said as I helped her unfasten her gown. "And liking it."

# CHAPTER 7

## ELENA DARCY

$\mathcal{D}$innertime came and we all made our way to Mr. Darcy's room. Desirous to be on time, Miss Elena Darcy met us in the hall before we knocked on his door.

"That is a lovely gown," Kitty complimented her.

"Thank you," Elena replied. "Yours is lovely as well."

"You are already making us like you," I administered, "for you are wonderfully on time."

"When people come to save you, the wisest thing to do is respect the clock."

Hearing our voices outside must have made the servants hear us, because Samuel opened the door.

"Ah, you all look lovely," Samuel noted.

"Thank you, Samuel," Georgiana said as we all entered. Mr. Darcy's quarters were larger and more spacious than ours, but that was to be expected. He took the room that we all could dine in together. Samuel led us to the dining room and Mr. Darcy was waiting for us there, looking as handsome as ever. He bowed to us, we all curtsied, and the servants brought the food to the tables as well as pulling out the chairs for us.

We thanked them and took our seats.

"You look excited," Elena said, looking at Kitty.

"It's because I am," Kitty said merrily. "I, too, have never been to Brighton before."

"Then there is something that I can offer you," Miss Elena said. "Having been here for such a time, I can lead you around Brighton and show you the best historic sites. Even in winter, this place still has much to offer. I know that I must appear as being presumptuous for recommending a holiday when in my... predicament. But moving forward in life is the only way that I can endure my situation."

"We do not criticize or despise your need to recover," I assured her. "Everyone should not spend their time living in the pain of the past. We are here to help you recover and the soonest that you do it, the better your future shall be."

"Thank you," she said, looking at me keenly. "You speak about my recovery with such confidence that I wonder what part it is that you will play in it." She looked at me, Jane and Kitty. "You are three sisters."

"Three of five," Jane said. "There is myself, then Elizabeth, Mary is our third sister, then Kitty, and Lydia is the last."

"You are three of five?"

"Yes. It is a number that often makes people's eyebrows raise."

"You are a lovely set." Then she turned to Georgiana. "You must be a delightful woman to have three sisters who wish to be your companion."

"Your error is my own mistake," Mr. Darcy said. "Due to all that has occurred so quickly, I have not had the time to explain it all. Miss Elizabeth and I are engaged. With my desire to have more of her family with us, I invited Miss Bennet and Miss Kitty as well."

"We have become great friends to Georgiana too, of course," Kitty inserted.

"Yes," Georgiana confirmed. "They started out as my brother's fiancée and sisters, and have turned into companions, as you say."

"Oh!" She turned to Darcy and me. "So, you two have found happiness with each other."

"Much to our surprise, yes," I answered, smiling.

Her eyes turned conspiratorial, as if she was attempting to unearth a secret.

"Congratulations. But I always love to know: how did you both meet? What was the wonderful circumstance that brought you both together?"

"We met at a ball where he refused to dance with me and thought me not worth the effort." I tossed Mr. Darcy a wry smile.

"And she spent months hating me for it," Mr. Darcy responded, equally unafraid of the truth.

Elena looked in between us.

"You are joking?"

"Not in the slightest," I said. "And when he says that I hated him for months, he is correct. I spent moments trying to find ways to punish him, too."

"Yes, she did," he replied, "and sometimes, she was successful. So, I would sometimes respond in kind."

"Yes. We worked to give each other pain."

Elena became fascinated.

"But you are engaged now?"

"Merrily so," I continued.

"And at what point did it transfer from contempt between each other to adoration?"

"I have a theory about that," I said, then I turned to Mr. Darcy. "You are at liberty to correct me, in case I am wrong. Unless your courage will falter under the prospect."

"I am not afraid of you," he administered, his eyes twinkling.

"You had better not be," I countered, "for it would not be that amusing if you were." Turning back to Elena, I explained. "My beauty was something that he long ago withstood. And as for my manners—my behavior to him was at least always bordering on the uncivil, and I never spoke to him without rather wishing to give him pain. Therefore, I cannot help but wonder if he admired me for my impertinence?"

"Your impertinence felt like it sprung from a liveliness of mind," Mr. Darcy pointed out.

"Thank you for the euphemism, but we both may as well call it impertinence at once. It was very little less. The fact is, that you were sick of civility, of deference, of officious attention. You were disgusted with the women who were always speaking and looking and thinking for *approbation* alone. I roused, and interested you, because I was so unlike them. Had you not been really amiable, you would have hated me for it. But in spite of the pains that you took to disguise yourself, your feelings were always noble and just. And in your heart, you thoroughly despised the persons who so assiduously courted you. There—I have saved you the trouble of accounting for it. And really, all things considered, I begin to think it perfectly reasonable. To be sure, you knew no actual good of me —but nobody thinks of that when they fall in love."

"Is that what I did?" Mr. Darcy asked me. Then he turned to Jane and Kitty. "Is that what I did?"

"Well," Kitty deduced, "that is the most logical theory I can see for how a man who once dismissed a woman's beauty finds himself so enraptured soon after."

"There is one thing that I wish to dispute," he argued.

"And what is that?" I asked.

"I did see good in you that did enhance your image in my eyes."

"What is this action? I must make sure to repeat it, in case my beauty once more becomes tolerable, but not handsome enough for consideration."

His smile was warm.

"I marry a woman who is not afraid of me."

"Yes, you do. Is that my good quality?"

"No. The first good quality that impressed me was when you looked after Miss Bennet, when she was sick at Netherfield."

"I was sick at another person's home," Jane explained to Elena, "and Elizabeth walked three miles to come and look after me"

"Three miles?" Elena repeated. "One mile would have been frightening to some women, two miles would have killed them, but you walked three, Miss Elizabeth?"

"Yes."

"No wonder my cousin was impressed."

"Very well," I said to Mr. Darcy. "I shall be content with that observation. You may make a virtue of my infamous walk, by all means. My good qualities are under your protection, and you are to exaggerate them as much as possible. And, in return, it belongs to me to find occasions of teasing and quarrelling with you as often as may be, because that may be the only way to keep you in love with me."

His eyes twinkled.

"You fight with me to give me what I want. In the history of married life, that may be the first."

"Then that makes us special."

We turned to Elena.

"Now you know how we fell in love."

This story made Elena lean back in her chair and analyze us.

"You argued with each other from the first day of your acquaintance and found love." She then made a comparison. "I was nothing short of agreeable to the man I met, and he agreeable to me, and it led to my predicament. This paints a very ironic approach to love. To get it, you must hate first? And if you love first, eventually it will lead to hate?"

"We are just as amazed at the paradox that is romance as well," I answered, "I can assure you."

"This paints a very strange image of how love can be approached. This now makes me become afraid of charm."

"And you ought to be," I encouraged. "Charm can be harmless, enjoyable, and even flattering. Yet, in the hands of the wrong man or woman, it is used to distract them from their base character."

"I can attest to that," Georgiana said, "for I too have suffered at the hands of the rake, and the contradictions are humbling. To be suspicious of kindness and affability, because it can appear as being untrustworthy—the pain of it."

"Precisely," Elena added. "For what of us women and men who wish to be agreeable and charming from the very beginning? What of us women who can't know how to be impertinent to a man and then see the good in him afterwards? What of us who are taken in from the very beginning? Are there no good examples of men in the world who can be charming in the beginning, as well as sincere?"

"If it helps, I have seen two such men," Jane said.

"Ah, not one, but two?" Elena smirked. "Plural."

We all laughed at that.

"Very well," Elena said after Jane told her a little bit about her past with Mr. Bingley and the Colonel. "You have persuaded me that there are still some men in the world who are charming and are sincere at the same time. I was beginning to feel like the mixture of sincerity and smoothness did not mix. Your Mr. Bingley and the Colonel give me hope." Then she turned to Mr. Darcy. "But you seem like a kind man. After all, these four women enjoy your company."

"I… I have not that talent of conversing easily with people that I have not met before," he continued. "I cannot always catch their style of talking and the tone of it. But once I begin to understand how they speak, and I grow more comfortable with them, I undergo an alteration of character. I become more open and approachable."

"You have been kind to me so far."

"My sister says that she trusts you, so I am willing to believe that she is correct."

"Your sister was kind to me when we first met." Elena smiled at Georgiana. "She did not care at all that our fathers refused to let us know each other. It was cruel, wasn't it? If I had the chance to have siblings, I would have felt less lonely. You and Georgiana were fortunate. You had each other." Then she looked at us Bennet sisters. "And you all must have been doubly fortunate. Five sisters. There must have never been a time where you felt lonely."

"And that drove our late father to distraction," I said. "He sometimes couldn't abide all the noise that we made."

"I believe that he liked the noise we made," Jane pointed out, "but he just took pleasure and saying the opposite."

"True. We humans sometimes say the opposite of how we feel." Here I looked at Mr. Darcy.

"And sometimes," Kitty added, "even when amongst a crowd, a person can feel lonely. Especially when one's thoughts are not like theirs. You can be amongst a group of people and still feel invisible."

"I confess that I felt like that at home sometimes," Elena said.

"Me too," Kitty added. Both women seemed like they enjoyed each other's similarities. I could easily see a bond growing between them.

"Is that what led to you seeking comfort elsewhere?" Mr. Darcy asked.

His observation cut through my musings and made us all sit up more alert.

Elena looked on him.

"Were your feelings of being invisible at home what inspired you to... make your plight?" he furthered.

"You speak in truths, cousin," Elena observed, "that is good. It means that you do not fear that I act in the same style. And you were insightful, because you might be very correct. Am I incorrect in assuming that you all know of my situation?"

"Due to their trust for us," I explained, "and that we will be staying with you, they thought it best to tell us your story. Please believe that your predicament will never be something we will expose."

"They will not say anything to anyone else," Georgiana assured her.

"And to convince you of our sincerity," I added, "I can offer proof. Months ago, our father passed away, and since then, we have been informed that we may lose our home because he had no male heirs. The only reason that we still have our estate is because no heir apparent has come forward to claim Longbourn. But if they exist, we shall be homeless and destitute. Therefore, we cling to our friends now, because our friends are the only fortune that we have left. The Darcys are our friends, and now that includes you. Even if we did not mean as we say, which we do, our situation would make us easy to take into your confidence. Because we would never abuse our friendships."

Elena released a rugged breath.

"I am sorry about your father," she said.

"Thank you," Jane said. "We still miss him."

"Well, through our tragedies, we unite. My plight was something that I did not put much thought into being past my own passions. I admit this. I only thought of the feelings that I had for him. But there is the possibility that, perhaps the internal need for acceptance and warmth prompted me to act as I did. And that internal need was a hole that was placed on the lack of affection that my home displayed. As improper as it is to speak ill of one's parents, they were not as they should have been."

"What were they like?" Kitty asked.

"They did not love each other. And my father, driven by a natural bitterness that came from his jealousy of your father," she said, looking from Mr. Darcy to Georgiana, "led to him never forgetting that he had to work, due to being the younger son. He married my mother for her wealth, she grew to know this, and they ended in despising each other. For one was the user, and the other was the one who had been used. Neither could forgive the other."

"And they really will not accept you now because of your conduct?" Georgiana asked. "Are they bereft of all proper feeling?"

"It is not in either of their natures to forgive. I thought I was going to escape that house of children's tears. But I had fooled myself. And so, here I am. I cannot thank you enough for coming to save me from my situation. Believe me when I say this, that I am humbled by it. You all do not seem apt to judge me harshly, so I think that you can believe that I do not intend to be any trouble. I just wish for some family now, and you are the only ones who seem to have any sort of familial devotion. How ironic it was that the only family who comes to protect me are the ones that I have little to no acquaintance with."

"I am not surprised," Kitty said. "Irony is one of Life's most powerful moods. She administers it randomly, so be happy that her mood was aimed your way when this all happened."

Elena looked at Mr. Darcy.

"You brought me four wonderful new friends."

"Be a good friend back to them, Miss Elena, and you will have repaid me for everything."

"And I let you down with our first bit of news," I compiled, "for the first thing that I bring to the table is a little bit of family complications that prevents us from whisking you away to safety as soon as you may wish. But, never fear, for once our first mission is complete, we shall look forward to distant horizons."

"Family complications?"

"There is a reason that we came to retrieve you from Brighton, rather than you coming to us."

"It is our youngest sister," Jane said, "Lydia Bennet. Miss Elena, are you well-acquainted with the regiment that is staying here?"

"Sadly yes," Elena answered. "I've seen them. The regiment is staying at the Old Ship Hotel. I've never met some of them. For that regiment is the regiment that my officer was supposed to join. He was a part of a unit of soldiers who were coming to add to the regiment's numbers. He sent me a letter to tell me to meet him here in Brighton. He was to check in with the Colonel, then once he had two days of reprieve, we would run away to Gretna Green. That being said, I am not acquainted with hardly anyone else in the regiment. After my situation, I did not wish to ever see a redcoat again."

"A natural reaction," I observed, "one redcoat can stir up memories of another redcoat. And we can't have that, now can we? The head of the regiment is named Colonel Forster, he has a wife, Mrs. Forster. Before coming to Brighton, they camped in Meryton, where we were from. Mrs. Forster took a liking to our youngest sister, Lydia, and invited her to come to Brighton. We learned of this in a letter that our sister sent. Once we discovered that you were in the same place that she was, the coincidence worked out well. It gave us another reason to come here and monitor her behavior."

"Oh," Elena said, biting into her food. "I cannot ignore the fact that you worry that she will turn out like me."

"No," I rushed out. "Our desire to be protective does not rest on us projecting your behavior onto her. Rather, it is us projecting our past knowledge of her onto her present situation and predicting her future behavior by it."

"Lydia is one of my closest friends," Kitty said, "but when it comes to officers, she has a significant weakness. I suppose that I do as well, but in the heat of the moment, we do not know if she is capable of taking the right course of action."

"We can assure you that your example is not what prompted our worry," Jane said, "but we were worried from the moment we finished reading the letter and knowing that Lydia was here, unfettered and unmonitored."

"Well, now that you are here," she concluded, "you can save

her from a fate similar to mine. But hopefully, nothing will happen, and she merely came to enjoy the officers' company and care for nothing more than that. It is possible."

"It is more possible for pigs to fly," I augmented before thinking. Elena chuckled.

The dinner ended and Elena left to go to her room, which was on a different floor than ours.

Kitty and Georgiana retired to their room, where they would no doubt talk about our new acquaintance.

Jane gave me another significant look.

"Lizzy, I shall check to make sure that there are no spiders again. But this time, I'll only take half a minute."

"Promise you will count the whole half a minute, and not just up to fifteen seconds?"

"I am not certain that I can promise that."

Jane went into the room and Darcy and I were left alone.

"Not enough time to drag me into your room," I teased.

"Do not ever doubt my physical powers, or my ruthlessness." Despite his words, his eyes twinkled.

"But Darcy, what did you think of your cousin?"

"What did you think of her?"

"As much as a woman cannot fully guarantee that they will never bring trouble to your life—too often trouble finds us no matter what we do—I do believe her. Whatever mistake she made, it was not the actions of a malicious woman, but a lonely one. She also possesses the Darcy frankness. How can I not admire that about her? And what of you?"

"She likes you all and you all like her. If she adheres to her promises, then I believe that she will be a nice addition."

"And what is it like to meet the cousin of your uncle who withdrew himself from your father's life?"

"That is the strange thing. I do not feel anything. In time, perhaps I shall feel something, but not right now."

"It is good to not feel a rush of emotions all at once. Doing so would give you an extreme case of mental indigestion, and we can't have that. Now, for the main thing I noticed. I admire your powers of deduction, for you noticed that she was lonely and that it was the source behind her actions. I was proud of you."

"Were you?"

"Yes. But I was proud in the proper amount. And when I say amount, I mean that I was proud of you enough to talk about it, but not so much that I will let you overpower my self-control."

"What did I say about not underestimating my powers of persuasion?"

"What did I say about my willingness to oppose you every now and again?" I challenged. "Oh, I believe this is that moment, Mr. Darcy. How will you challenge me?"

His eyes turned fierce again.

"I'll tell you what I am about to do."

He could not finish his sentence because Jane emerged again.

"That was no longer than thirty seconds," Darcy and I said in unison again. We both gave each other another look.

"We have got to stop doing that," I urged.

"We wouldn't if you always let me speak first," he intoned.

"Good luck with that dream," I retorted.

"There was one spider," Jane informed me.

"What?" I asked.

"Actually, no," she said, "I found no spider at all. Now the hour grows late."

I turned to Mr. Darcy and curtsied.

"Mr. Darcy, I must bid you a goodnight."

"Good night, Miss Elizabeth."

I went into our room and Jane closed the door behind me.

"Jane, if you are wishing to succeed at being the best chaperone in the world, then I give you full marks. But you do irk me."

"Then that means I am the very best," Jane pointed out.

I looked around the room.

"Jane, tell me the truth. Did you really find a spider?"

"No matter what I say, you will never believe me."

"You did find a spider, didn't you? And you're just sparing my feelings."

"Lizzy, do not ask anymore. I know how you get with thinking about these sorts of things. Just think happy thoughts."

Giving in, we talked only about Elena Darcy as we undressed for bed. Both she and I agreed that, as far as first impressions went, we liked the new Miss Darcy who was in our midst.

# CHAPTER 8

## NOT SO GREAT AN ESCAPE

*T*he next day brought another day to become acquainted with Miss Elena Darcy. But as I warned her before, we were going to have to enter the lion's den. We all had partaken breakfast in the main dining hall when I began.

"Miss Elena, I am sorry, but we wish to inquire after our sister at the Old Ship Hotel," I said. "If you do not wish to come with us, then I understand. But something tells me that you might wish to do the opposite."

"You think so?" she asked me.

"If I am correct about your nature, then I believe so."

"You analyzed my character."

"It is a tendency of mine to study characters. I have been wrong before. Forgive me if I am wrong about you."

"I am curious to see what you have deduced about me."

"Naturally you do not wish to encounter any redcoats, because it may stir up bad memories. Yet, you do not strike me as the sort who wishes to run away from anything for very long. Therefore, this prospect might annoy you in the beginning, but you will not let it weaken your spirit."

"Besides," Kitty encouraged, "you do not know if the nefarious officer told anyone else about your journey. The incident may very well have died within us and him."

"Yes," Georgiana encouraged. "I think all will be well."

"I confess," Elena said, "the idea of being a coward does not feel proper." Elena looked around at us and then at Mr. Darcy. "I feel as if our family is always having to rise to a courage, even if we don't feel it."

"Call it the Darcy pride," Mr. Darcy stated.

"Very well, Miss Elizabeth, Miss Kitty and Georgiana. I shall defer to your belief in me. Besides, there is no chance of Mr. Wilson being there. So, what have I to fear? So, your sister's name is Lydia, yes?"

"Yes," Jane confirmed.

"I hope that she likes me."

"She likes redcoats," I clarified. "Since none of us is wearing one, she will only talk to us because we are family."

"I have a red dress."

"Maybe that will help."

"It wouldn't help, would it?"

I chuckled. "Not in the slightest."

---

"Jane, Lizzy, and Kitty!" Lydia shrieked as we met her in the hotel. She had been sitting with Mrs. Forster, a few other women, and lots of officers. They were dining in the hotel's dining hall and there was a general sense of merriment.

"How are you doing?" Kitty asked Elena, holding her arm. "Still afraid of the color red?"

"It is a color that I suppose no one has the right to hate for long," Elena said, looking around. "I think I can find it within myself to be agreeable. But no more than that."

Lydia ran up to us and hugged us all. Kitty's hug was the grandest as both sisters hugged longer and twirled around in the process.

"You have come for the fun of it," Lydia said, "and to see me! That makes sense, but I admit that I have been far too merry to miss any of you. I am happy that you are here, because this is the place to get husbands! Jane and Lizzy, you will be old maids very soon unless we do something about it."

"I still expound on the idea of how old does one have to be to be regarded as an old maid?" I asked. "For every year, the age seems to get younger and younger. Pretty soon, old maid will stand for anyone who is over fifteen years old. What a scary world that will be. And Lydia, you are so profuse in your speech that you haven't introduced yourself to our new acquaintances and greeted old ones. Lydia, Mr. Darcy is here."

Lydia turned to Mr. Darcy and curtsied.

"Mr. Darcy, you have brought my sisters to me. I feel like I shall laugh."

"Why?" Mr. Darcy asked, his face like stone. He still did not like her.

"And you have not changed! One time, I wondered if I could extract three words from you. And I still have not succeeded."

"True."

I bit my lip, amused.

"And," I continued, "this is Mr. Darcy's sister, Miss Georgiana Darcy. And this is their cousin, Miss Elena Darcy."

"It is a pleasure to make your acquaintance," Miss Elena said as they all curtsied to each other.

"Miss Lydia, I have heard so much about you," Georgiana said.

"And yet no one ever told me that you have met my sisters. Jane, Lizzy and Kitty, you have left me in the dark. What a joke! And with gowns like that, I am sure that the officers will fall in love with the both of you. I can also get beaus for my sisters, too."

"Thank you for my share of the offer," I said, "but I prefer my own fortune."

"You still are too severe, Lizzy."

"When it comes from you, I take that as a compliment of the highest regard."

"Now, come and speak to Mrs. Forster and the Colonel!" Lydia said, pulling us all to the company. "I want everyone to see how much you all care about me by coming."

"Lydia, we have come to stay with you for a time here in Brighton," Jane explained. "Then, after a few days, we wish for you to return to town with us."

"I can't," Lydia scoffed. "I was invited, and I have more fun here than at home. Sometimes I wonder if I would be happy anywhere else ever again."

"But you must," Jane urged. "We will not leave until you come with us."

"Then we will stay in Brighton forever. Mrs. Forster and Colonel Forster, look who has come to see me!"

Accepting our fate, we approached the couple and it was not unpleasant. In truth, I did always find the Colonel and his wife to be pleasant people, so it was nice to see them again... until the inevitable moment occurred next.

"Mr. Wickham will be happy to see you," Mrs. Forster said, then she turned to another group of soldiers that were on the other side of the room. "Mr. Wickham, come here. We have friends for you to meet."

My insides froze, and then I quickly looked at Mr. Darcy and Miss Georgiana. From the other room, an officer untangled himself from his friends and walked up to us—only to halt immediately when he beheld all of us.

"Mr. Wickham," I spoke first, to smooth the way, "it's a pleasure to see you again."

Mr. Wickham only had a second to recover from his shock of seeing me and the rest.

"Miss Elizabeth," he faltered, "this is an incredible surprise."

"I can well believe it. As you see, my sisters Miss Bennet and Miss Kitty are with me. And you remember Mr. Darcy and Miss Darcy, of course."

Mr. Wickham looked quickly at Mr. Darcy and then his face fell on Georgiana.

"Mr. Wickham." Georgiana curtsied. "You appear to be doing well."

"Miss—Miss Darcy," he nearly stuttered, then bowed. "You are as lovely as ever."

"You still flatter."

"Once more. As always."

I could feel the hatred and contempt radiating off Mr. Darcy. His scowl was perhaps tearing at Mr. Wickham's composure. What we were watching was a redcoat of a peacock who was flaunting his feathers to distract people from his uncertainty and panic.

"And," I continued, "we have a new acquaintance for you. This is Miss Elena Darcy, Mr. Darcy and Miss Georgiana's cousin."

"Cousin?" Mr. Wickham questioned. "From one of the late Mr. Darcy's brothers?"

"Yes. Mr. Lionel Darcy is my father."

"It is a pleasure to make your acquaintance. If I may be so bold, I would determine that you have elegance of the Darcy family in your person. Now that I look at you, I wonder that I did not see it immediately."

"I am fine with people never making assumptions of me to begin with," Miss Elena said, "so I am happy that you did not detect it."

"Wit," he observed with a chuckle, "that is always welcome." Then he gave me a look. "Yes, it is."

Turning to Mrs. Forster, Wickham found his footing at how to untangle himself from this most awkward situation.

"Now, I daresay that I am an intrusion," he apologized, "for Miss Lydia's family will long to speak to her in confidence. I would be in the way of that."

With another bow, he excused himself.

"Well," I whispered to Mr. Darcy, "at least he had the good graces to run away at the soonest opportunity."

"He was always good at running," Mr. Darcy retorted.

"What?" Lydia gasped after Wickham. "My family can have nothing to say that you are not allowed to overhear!"

"Wickham spoke well," Jane added, "for there *are* things that family should speak about in secret."

"Well, if you are going to tell me that mama says that she loves me, I know already," Lydia said. "Tell her that I love her and that I am having the time of my life. Aren't we having fun, Mrs. Forster?"

"Yes," Mrs. Forster agreed, happily. "Lydia and I cannot go more than five minutes without laughing about something."

"How can we go back to the country after finding so much joy by the shore?" Lydia compiled, taking Mrs. Forster's hand. "When life is so pleasant, I cannot go back to the dullness that we used to always be suffering under."

"Our lives were not dull at home, but peaceful," Jane pointed out.

"I will never agree with you."

"Miss Lydia," Mr. Darcy cut in, "your sisters came expressly to see you, to speak to you about family matters. It would be indelicate of you to disappoint them."

Lydia gasped.

"I made you say more than two words!"

Mr. Darcy closed his eyes, groaning inwardly.

"And he is right," I supported. "We really do want to speak to you about so many things and tell you how we have been."

"Miss Lydia," Colonel Forster said, "you must speak to your family. For they have come expressly to see you."

"Oh, very well!" Lydia gave in. "I just am afraid that all you will talk about is how sad we are about Longbourn."

"Thank you, Colonel," Kitty said to him, giggling. "She is better at listening to you than to us."

Lydia was compelled to follow us to a private parlor at the end of the hall.

Despite myself, I felt compelled to turn and look over my shoulder. When I did, I saw Mr. Wickham glaring at me from the end of the room.

Did he have a reason to be upset? Perhaps he did.

---

When we closed the door behind us, Lydia threw up her hands.

"I cannot believe it of you, Jane, Lizzy and Kitty! You were so cold to Mr. Wickham, and it makes no sense. Lizzy, didn't he used to be a favorite of yours?"

I rolled my eyes, embarrassed and thoroughly vexed that she brought that up.

"Believe me, he wasn't. Enjoying a gentleman's company does not make him a favorite, but a common acquaintance."

"You're lying. I believe you are merely jealous of me for always being in the presence of officers. Kitty, I know that you must be envious."

"I know I should be, but not really," Kitty replied, innocently and without any pretense. She even seemed surprised for saying it. "I suppose that redcoats don't impress me as much as they used to."

"Kitty, how can you say such a thing?"

"Believe me, I am just as surprised as you are! But I honestly do not care a jot." Kitty turned to Elena to explain. "Back home, Lydia and I were partners in the act of always seeing the officers and enjoying partaking in a reel. Some may scoff, but I meant no harm in liking their company."

"There is never anything wrong with enjoying one's fellow man," Elena pointed out. "Too many people walk through life viewing their fellow creatures as merely strangers to the grave."

"Yes. Then I went to London, and I suppose a wider acquaintance with the ways of the world has changed me—and I didn't notice till now."

"Kitty, stay with me!" Lydia implored. "We can be as we once were. Running free and dancing at balls every night. And Miss Elena and Miss Georgiana, you will have fun as well. The officers will love you both. I have quite given up on you both, Jane and Lizzy. You are too serious."

"Us, too serious?" I echoed, raising an eyebrow. "I'd answer that, but that would only make you happy. For some reason, I like the idea of not letting you win. But you have your wish. Because we are staying." Then I walked up to her, my eye satirical, and with powers of intimidation. "We shall be here to inquire after you every day, we shall find out who you danced with at balls—we may even go to some of them and make you stand up with us, one of your sisters."

Lydia looked alarmed.

"You wouldn't dare!"

"Now who's the serious one? You look like you've never laughed a day in your life."

Lydia looked at Kitty.

"Kitty, do not let them do this to me."

Kitty laughed.

"Lydia," she augmented, "Lizzy is clearly joking."

"Am I though?" I continued, amused. "Perhaps I am. Or perhaps I am not. But here is the bargain that I shall make. Lydia. We will not hound you every day if you promise to return home with us when we choose to leave for London. But if you refuse, I will literally do everything in my power to keep officers from asking you to dance ever again while I am here."

"You do not have that power."

"Do I not? Mr. Darcy, do I have the power?"

"Yes," Mr. Darcy said, his tone heavier than ever and his face like stone. "And so do I."

Hearing that Mr. Darcy would interfere was enough to make Lydia feel the gravity of our threat.

"Why are you all being so cruel to me?" she asked. "What have I done to make you all so upset?"

"You did nothing," Jane assured her. "We are doing this to protect you. We are worried that you are not being properly looked after."

"Colonel Forster and Mrs. Forster look after me just fine."

"But family always helps to be beside you," Miss Darcy added. "Why are you so averse to them being here?"

"Oh well, I suppose that it must be, if you put it like that."

"So," I said, "do you agree?"

Lydia rolled her eyes.

"When will you leave? Because I don't want to leave so soon. Remember, I was invited by Mrs. Forster as her particular friend. It would be inappropriate for me to leave after a short visit."

"Our stay is not fully determined," Mr. Darcy answered, "but perhaps we shall stay no more than a fortnight."

"Only two weeks?" Lydia gasped. "But I shall miss out on so much."

"Lydia," I furthered, "our bargain? Remember, Mr. Darcy and I can frighten anyone away—that includes officers. Look at my fiancé; who is more imposing than him?"

Mr. Darcy didn't smirk, but I could tell from the twinkling of his eyes, that he was most flattered.

"Oh, very well," Lydia whined. "I'll agree. But please try and stay more than two weeks. For me."

"We shall consider it," I offered. "But we can make no promises. But please believe that we are happy to see you."

"I find that hard to believe."

Once again, she rolled her eyes and left the room.

Turning to Elena, I gave her a shrewd look.

"Still wish that you had sisters?" I asked her.

"Yes, actually," she remarked, very amused. "Interminable foolishness is infinitely preferable to interminable silence. Say what you will about you group of sisters, you make life interesting."

We left the parlor and went to the Colonel and Mr. Forster to thank them again for inviting our sister and to offer our farewells. When we did, we were in for another shock.

An officer who just arrived was standing in front of them, handing his orders over to the Colonel.

"Colonel Fitzwilliam!" Jane extoled.

There, amongst the group, was Colonel Fitzwilliam.

Seeing us, he turned, removed his hat, bowed and his expression was welcoming, but also apprehensive.

"Richard!" Georgiana almost laughed. "This was unexpected."

"Georgiana and Miss Bennet," he began, "and your sisters, and Darcy. I apologize at our sudden meeting and I assure you that I have not come by design. I was given orders to come here and investigate a certain matter of an officer who defected from my regiment. And now I am reporting to Colonel Forster."

"Really?" Jane said. "What happened?"

Colonel Fitzwilliam's face relaxed, happy to see that Jane was willing to still be comfortable in his presence.

"I promise that I shall explain everything further when the time is proper."

"So, you are all acquainted?" Colonel Forster asked.

"Yes," Mr. Darcy explained. "Colonel Fitzwilliam is our cousin," he said, nodding to Georgiana. "And, in a distant way, he is also Miss Elena's cousin as well."

"Miss Elena?" Colonel Fitzwilliam asked, then he turned to

Elena, who was the only face in the group that was unknown to him.

"Richard," Mr. Darcy continued, "this is our cousin, Miss Elena Darcy. She is my uncle's daughter, on my father's side."

"Miss Elena Darcy." Colonel Fitzwilliam bowed. "It is a pleasure to meet you."

She curtsied to him. She opened her mouth to speak but closed it when she observed how he was looking at her. Indeed, Colonel Fitzwilliam was looking at her in a fixed way—and unless I was mistaken, it was not a look of love or attraction. It was a look of perplexity.

"Richard?" Georgiana asked, and this woke him up. Colonel Fitzwilliam blinked and he returned to us.

"Yes, forgive me. I have begun this introduction in the worst sort of way."

"There are worse ways to begin something," Kitty helped him. "You are forgiven, Colonel."

Colonel Fitzwilliam exhaled, grateful at Kitty for shielding him.

"And Miss Kitty saves me from myself," he responded. "Miss Elena, see how between my cousins and the Bennet sisters, you are in a company that you will adore."

"I have been shown this already, so you and I are quite in agreement."

"Kitty!" Lydia cried, grabbing Kitty's hand. "You never told me that Mr. Darcy had a cousin in regimentals."

"I did," Kitty said, "I wrote of it. You must have forgotten. Colonel Fitzwilliam, this is our youngest sister, Lydia."

"Miss Lydia Bennet," Colonel Fitzwilliam bowed again. "You have the bearing of your sisters. I feel as if I should know you anywhere."

"We all have the Bennet look, except for our other sister, Mary. She looks nothing like the rest of us."

"When I see you all together in a set, I shall see the truth of that, I believe." Then he turned to Darcy. "Darcy, forgive me, but I need to speak to you for a moment on a matter of business that is of the highest importance."

The Colonel gave Darcy such a significant look that Darcy felt compelled to give in. Taking one last look at us, he excused himself, saying that he wouldn't be gone for long and then he walked away with the Colonel.

Now that we women were alone, Colonel Forster took the opportunity to be gallant.

"Now, we have officers aplenty," he began, "so who can we introduce you to?"

"Anyone and everyone who is willing to be pleasant," Miss Elena Darcy pointed out. "I rely on kindness right now."

"That can be arranged."

"I know the perfect people," Lydia declared, pulling Kitty, Jane, Elena, and me along. "Denny and Carter will love to meet you and Miss Darcy. Come along, come along!"

She led us all to the other side of the room where Captain Carter and Denny were with a group of soldiers. Lydia introduced them to Elena and Georgiana, and we all were able to feel like ourselves again. For say what you will, but Denny and Carter were always gentlemanlike men, without being gentlemen. Therefore, I had no qualms in being congenial to them.

After a brief while, Lydia and Kitty dominated the conversation, Jane stood next to Georgiana and they were speaking to each other. Without knowing it, I found myself on the outskirts of the group.

From behind me, I felt a figure looming.

"You find your way to Brighton," the familiar voice said behind me. "Is it by accident, or by design?"

I turned and Mr. Wickham was standing so close to me that very little could have fit between us.

"Accident or design?" I repeated, whispering. "Even if I told you the truth, would you believe me?"

Our entire conversation was spoken low, to ensure that no one overheard us.

"Perhaps I would not," he admitted. "I cannot tell what my feelings are at present. They are such a mixture of confusion."

"Let me see if I understand your soul. You are happy to see me, but also, you hate the idea of seeing me. And you have so much to say, but you know that you will not say anything correctly, because internally, you are all in disarray."

He raised an eyebrow.

"You know what I am feeling."

"I guessed. I am happy to see that I am right."

"You should not be. For, with every second, my feelings are leaning more toward resentment."

"Be careful, Mr. Wickham," I said, looking at Georgiana, "I've seen the results of your resentment."

"I feel regret over my past actions, but I refuse to accept, or respect, that you held my past actions over my head."

"You lied as well as slandered the woman that you lied about," I insisted. "How can you blame me for being logical?"

"Because I was hoping to change my ways when we married. And then you turned from me the second that you saw my flaws. That makes it very evident that you never loved me from the very beginning. For rarely do people care about other's flaws when they are in love."

"You are correct," I admitted. "When I first met you, I was charmed by you, but my heart was not fully touched. Perhaps it was my vanity that appealed to you, because you nourished it. I did like you, Mr. Wickham, but I am not certain that it was ever love."

His eyes burned.

"That is a lie. You did love me. You just forgot it when Mr. Darcy exposed my past. You will love me again, Miss Elizabeth. Yes, you will love me again."

His tone, look, and insistence, actually frightened me in that moment. I wondered if I ever actually knew him at all.

"I choose what my heart does. You insist on me loving you when I am in the company of the woman you once almost eloped with."

"I do feel abominable about that now. Please tell Miss Georgiana that I apologize for my actions. I see that I was wrong then, and I was wrong for lying about it."

"You defamed her and her brother when you were the culprit."

"I was younger, an idiot, and I was so determined to make

everyone like me in Hertfordshire, that I was desperate. Tell Miss Darcy this. For I have not the right to tell her myself."

I looked at Georgiana and was saddened to say that she saw us talking. I had to keep her safe.

"I will tell her," I assured him, "but your presence still hurts her. Please, give her less pain now."

"Very well. But consider my words before I go."

"Mr. Wickham," I gave way. Despite that I held no remorse for not accepting his proposal, I still did not want to hurt him. But he needed to know this. "I take no pleasure in telling you this, despite what you may believe. But you must know. Mr. Darcy has asked for my hand in marriage, and I have accepted him."

This announcement had a marked effect on Mr. Wickham. His visage darkened. His manner lost all easiness. In that moment, I felt like a mask was slipping off his face and I saw the creature underneath.

"You what?" he hissed, bitter.

"You heard me, and you must believe what I say. I love him and we are to be married. Mr. Wickham, please be happy for me."

"I despise you," he replied, enraged.

"You said that you would walk away from me, for Georgiana's sake. Now walk away."

"With all eagerness."

"Then do so," came a thunderous voice behind us. "And do not vex my fiancée with your company."

We both turned and Mr. Darcy returned, with Colonel Fitzwilliam standing behind him.

Both men glared at Mr. Wickham, who buckled under the weight of their contempt.

"Yes," Mr. Wickham said, "of course."

With alacrity, he walked away from us and departed from the dining hall.

Protectively, Mr. Darcy grabbed my arm, placed it in his and announced that it was time to go.

"Come back and see me!" Lydia called. "As long as you try to be merry and not so dour."

Mr. Darcy took Georgiana's arm in his other one. Colonel

Fitzwilliam offered Kitty and Jane his arms as well, and Mr. Darcy gestured for Miss Elena to follow us.

We left the Old Ship Hotel, and the Colonel saw us to the carriage.

"If my company will not be too irksome," the Colonel said, standing with us in front of the hotel, "Might I visit you all at the Grand Brighton while I stay here?"

We all turned to Jane, out of instinct. Before any of us could answer, she decided to be quick and cover our blunder.

"Of course, you may visit," she responded. "It is always nice to meet with excellent friends."

He smiled at her, glad that she did not want him to be on the other side of the world from us.

"Thank you."

"We dine for supper at 7 o'clock," Darcy informed him. "Come then."

"I would be delighted." He nodded to us all, to Jane significantly. "And Miss Elena Darcy, it is always nice to meet more family."

"Yes, it is."

He left us and went back into the hotel. As we walked back to the Grand Brighton, Mr. Darcy held my arm, but I was not fit for conversation.

Mr. Wickham's words and expressions still filled my mind.

When thinking of Mr. Wickham's first, second and third impressions, he is described as being charming, handsome and superior to the rest of his sex.

After a fourth, fifth and sixth impression, he is revealed to be inconstant, a rake, his sweet words hollow, and he is a liar.

Now I was at the seventh impression, and just when I thought that I knew him, I didn't.

There is a darkness in all of us, but since his is so well concealed, his is the most frightening.

I saw that dark side of him... and it was hideous.

# CHAPTER 9

## JUDGE & JEALOUSY

*a*s we returned to the hotel, Darcy insisted that we each take some time to rest and go down to dine together in an hour.

When we reached his room again, Jane was content to give us a whole minute this time, under her perpetual excuse of protecting me from encountering any eight-legged creatures. Once the door was closed, I turned to Mr. Darcy, about to compliment him for how he stood by me as a united front in Lydia's case, when I saw him look on me with unmistakable rage. With a swiftness that I never knew he possessed, he grabbed my arm, pulled me into his room, and closed the door behind us.

"You have bested me this time," I gasped, breathing in heavily. "I was not even given a chance to put up a fight."

"Because I am not amused." He wielded on me with a fury. "Elizabeth, how could you?"

"How could I? What are you referring to?"

"You let Mr. Wickham talk to you? How could you!"

"I did not mean to. He approached me!"

"Then you should have ignored him!"

"Sometimes by doing so, it exposes us to looking rude. Would you like me to cause such an image?"

"I do not care what it looks like. How could you hurt me like that?"

This outburst was so random and took me by surprise that I could not censor my reactions.

"I never hurt you! And in what way could you even have deduced that? I confronted him about his lack of shame in addressing me when Georgiana was right there. I forced him to confront his horrible behavior to you and your sister, I promised that I would relay his apologies to her, and I told him of our engagement."

Despite saying this, it was as if I had not, because Darcy only remained angry as he moved away from me.

"Do you still love him?" he asked me.

His question hung in the air and cast a spell on me. I was horrified at his question.

"What did you just ask?" I repeated.

"Since I am incapable of stuttering at this time, I believe that you did hear me. Do you—or did you ever—love him?"

"Darcy, tell me this now. Is this outburst of yours springing from a place of jealousy?"

"Should it be?"

"No, it should not be!" I exclaimed, upset that he even proposed this. "What power could make you think that I would love a man while being devoted to you? When have I ever appeared inconstant to you? I yield to you, I sometimes lose all self-command, and never have I shown preference for him since we became friends. Yes, I enjoyed his company from the beginning, but it was NEVER love. I found a comfort in him, which helped me recover from the coldness from you."

He turned to me, disturbed in this.

"If you had been kinder to me from the beginning, and had acted on your feelings sooner, then I never would have believed his charm and lies, because you would have protected me from them. But no. I was left unguarded and ignorant on something, while you never displayed any particular regard for me. I was wrong to believe him and not notice the indelicacy of his behavior. But my relationship with him was shaped by you. And it ended, because of you. I chose you and not him. And now you do not trust me."

"Elizabeth…"

"No. You do me an unkindness, and I will not stand by and let you rail at me for that."

There was a knock on our door.

"Elizabeth," Jane said, "are you in there?"

"Coming!" I called.

"Come out immediately," Jane said firmly, but simply.

I went to the door and then turned back to him.

"When I was speaking to Mr. Wickham, I did nothing but point out to him how he wronged you and your sister. And I was about to tell you how much it meant when you stood by me and chastised Lydia. I was proud of you. Now, I don't know what I feel."

I opened the door. Jane took a look at both our faces and saw that we were grieved. I slammed the door behind me and gave her a look.

"Never get engaged," I warned her.

I went to our room and she followed.

After I told her all that happened, Jane was pensive. At last, she spoke.

"First, I now know that I cannot leave you both alone in the hallway," she began. "I was being too soft before. Second, Elizabeth, I am so sorry that he said all that. He ought to trust you."

"Thank you."

"It would have been more proper for him to have calmly asked you about your transaction with Mr. Wickham, and then formed his opinions about it afterwards."

"Yes!" I declared, pacing back and forth. "He ought to have done that, but did he? No! And he wondered if I loved Mr. Wickham. Honestly!"

"While you have every reason to be angry," Jane furthered, "I would advise you not to continue so, because I now can see where Mr. Darcy's mind was at."

I stopped and stared at her, incredulous.

"You do?"

"Yes," she continued. "Your fiancé was not speaking rationally or kindly to you because he *wasn't* thinking. He was *feeling*. Seeing you speak to Mr. Wickham incited his anger because he was possessive, jealous and immediately wished to lash back."

"And it led to him lashing out upon me."

"Because he cares. He's in love with you, and it leads to him being overprotective, and paranoid. I have learned that love can create both of those sad sensations. You are right to be angry, but I urge you to calm down and reflect. He recalls a time when you spoke warmly of Mr. Wickham, and no matter how much he tries to show otherwise, he is not stone. Mr. Darcy is human."

Looking out of the window at the busy street below, I considered her words.

"Yes," I agreed, "he is more human than people realize."

"Perhaps you need to speak to him about if he is still insecure on that score. Maybe your past friendship with Mr. Wickham still hurts him and he cannot forget it. After all, wouldn't you? Imagine if Mr. Darcy blatantly favored a woman, that woman slandered you, he believed it, then you displayed your love for him, and he responded by accusing you of those false crimes, while mentioning the woman who he was close to. Would you be jealous if you walked up and saw them conversing?"

I closed my eyes, seeing the sense of this.

"Yes, you are quite right. I wish that I was as smart as you in this case."

"I am not the one who is in love with him. You are. Because of such, I am the only one who has the ability of being rational, because my heart is not involved."

"But your heart is involved elsewhere," I said. "We have not had the chance to speak about this new development. What was it like to see the Colonel again?"

Jane released a long, slow breath.

"Thank you for worrying about me, but I assure you that there is no need. I cling to my purpose, am not nervous, and as you see, I can meet Colonel Fitzwilliam with tranquility."

"I marveled at that."

"So did I," she replied. "Even I was amazed with myself. I had come here to run away, and suddenly, there is the Colonel. But rather than be alarmed, I faced the situation and was not afraid of seeing him again."

"Does seeing him again make you lean more toward him as a choice at all?"

"I am happy to see him, and I have not forgotten my love for him, but no, I am still adamant. I hurt one by choosing the other. I'd rather hurt both a little, than one a lot. Also, while it is bewitching to find all of one's happiness through being wed, I still feel like I have a few more experiences to undergo before I feel inclined to marry anyone. I need a little more time to wonder about the woman that I am."

I gave her a warm smile. "I know who Jane Bennet is. She is my perfect older sister."

Jane blushed.

"But I am not sure that Jane Bennet knows who she is sometimes," she said about herself. "Never fear. I am happy right now. And that is all that matters to me."

"But now I need to know what the right course of action is. Should I wait till Mr. Darcy sees me again to make peace, or should I go to him?"

"That is difficult indeed."

"Yes. Should I be proactive or reactive? That is the question."

"Think of the other times when you misjudged each other. How did it get resolved before?"

"One came to the other and hoped for the best." I stopped and thought on us all. "When I berated him for his past, he didn't leave Hunsford Parsonage, but confronted the matter and I listened. When I came to London, wanting to make amends, I sent him a letter and he came. We *both* have gone to each other to end any miscommunication, rather than let tension and prejudice thrive."

It all had made sense now! Everything became clear.

"It doesn't matter which one of us is the first to make amends," I said. "As long as one of us does."

I looked in the mirror to make sure that I looked presentable. Next, I gave her a shrewd look.

"I am not afraid of spiders right now so you can keep the door open and listen for us, so that we are never without a chaperone."

"Well, go on then!" she encouraged me.

I opened the door and stepped out of it... only to be met by Mr. Darcy coming out of his room as well.

Our eyes locked on each other and we froze.

"I was coming to see you," I explained.

"As was I," he replied.

I closed the door behind me mostly but left it slightly ajar.

"We both came out at the same time," I pointed out.

"Another moment of us acting in unison."

"For the first time, I am happy that we did so." I took a few steps toward him. "I love you."

His face relaxed and his eyes turned gentle, losing the worried expression that was there a second ago.

"I love you as well."

Walking up to me, he took my hand in his. I raised his hand up to my lips and kissed it. When I separated my lips from his palm, I looked at his fingers.

"Your hands are beautiful," I professed. "I do not know how I never noticed it before."

Finally, I looked up at him and his expression was all tenderness.

"Might I…"

"You may," I allowed.

Once more, he leaned down, and we kissed. The depth of our affection had done the trick. There were no apologies needed. We had both forgiven each other, and that was the end of it. When all strife had ended, we had returned to our most fortunate state: we were no longer clinging to misunderstandings.

After a minute of expressing our passion, our lips separated. It was as if we suspected that we were not alone. Instinctively, we turned our heads and Elena Darcy was standing there, with a gown in her hands.

"Oh, you must excuse me. I just came down to get Kitty's advice on if this gown was suitable to wear for dinner this evening.

Since Colonel Fitzwilliam is coming, I want to make a good first impression."

"Oh," I answered, a little breathless.

"Right," Mr. Darcy voiced.

Faith, neither of us knew what we were about. Immediately, we separated and went into our rooms. Lord knows what Elena thought of us.

When I went into the room, I leaned against the door and covered my mouth. I saw Jane sitting on her bed, biting her lip.

"You heard all of what happened, didn't you?" I asked.

"I tried not to listen, but it was a little impossible to not overhear."

"No matter. No one in life has the right to always be perfect."

# CHAPTER 10

## THE COLONEL & HIS MISSION

At six o'clock, Mr. Darcy waited downstairs for Colonel Fitzwilliam's arrival, and the Colonel did not disappoint. He met us all in Darcy's quarters, the servants brought in the food and we began to eat.

"So," Colonel Fitzwilliam began, "how are you all enjoying Brighton? I know that it is still the winter, and this is not the season to see it at its best, but at least it is not as busy, so you can have a large portion of it all to yourselves."

"We have just arrived," Georgiana explained, "so we have not gotten the chance to see much of it."

"If the chance arises," Elena administered, "I will guide them around the city and show them the best of the place."

"It's always nice to have a guide," Colonel Fitzwilliam said, "because I am quite useless in that regard."

"As for the other part of it," Kitty compiled, "yes, we may have the place to ourselves, in part, but sometimes a crowd can add atmosphere to a place. But since we are all together, I think you may be right in this case. Unless we count the officers, but who knows how often we are going to be in their company. Which makes me ask, how long will we have you for company? For business must tug at your redcoat."

"Business is why I am here," Colonel Fitzwilliam said, "which truly IS the primary reason for my coming. I was fortunate that my odious task brought me to family, rather than taking me from it. Especially now that my family circle is growing."

He nodded to Elena.

"I have heard about your situation and I feel sorry for it. For all three Darcy brothers to not wish for their children to know each other is a significant loss. Nothing is better than family ties."

"As long as those ties do not strangle," I pointed out, to which everyone laughed.

"And these ties do not hurt at all," Elena assented. "You are correct, Colonel. This is the main benefaction to my circumstance. Because of it, I have had to reach out to family that I usually was not allowed to. This situation can even argue that through misfortune, I have become wealthier."

"Wisely said," Colonel Fitzwilliam praised.

As we ate, Jane decided that it was proper to speak to him.

"Colonel, you mentioned that you came here on business, but your regiment is still in London. What is this business that brought you here? You mentioned a defection."

Colonel Fitzwilliam looked apprehensive.

"It is a heavy subject that I wonder if it is proper to talk about with lovely ladies at dinner."

"They are lovely, but sturdy," Mr. Darcy augmented, "and I have gotten so far into the habit of telling them the absolute truth of things that it would be inconsiderate of me to deny them information. Besides, what you told me earlier is something I felt that it was your right to tell them yourself. And if you weren't going to tell them, then I am going to when you leave. Either way, they shall end the evening knowing the truth."

Colonel Fitzwilliam leaned back in his chair, his eyes glowing from the candlelight that was reflected in them.

"Miss Elizabeth, you are quite the good influence on my cousin."

"Thank you but call on us again in five years. If I am still a good influence, then I shall full accept your compliment."

"If it helps you," Mr. Darcy said to Colonel Fitzwilliam, "they know all about Elena's misfortune."

"They do?"

"Yes," Miss Elena said, "we have no secrets here. I was the one to lay my soul bare, voluntarily."

"Very brave. Well, I come with further news on that subject. The officer who was the worthless libertine that you knew, Miss Elena, his name is Mr. James Wilson."

"Yes," Miss Elena said.

"Well, when he was so busy being the worst of rakes and taking advantage of your heart, I am going to assume that he neglected to mention that he is an officer—in my regiment."

We all stopped what we were doing and looked at the Colonel.

"Truly?" Jane asked.

"Yes," Colonel Fitzwilliam continued. "I am afraid that the sorry excuse for an officer was under my command."

"Oh," Elena observed. "So, when he eloped with me, you must have been given the news."

"It wasn't just that, but he defected to run away with you. Therefore, he is guilty of two things: acting like the worst of mercenary libertines, as well as being a deserter. When you refused to marry him here in Brighton, his actions became known to Colonel Forster, who detained him. Then he wrote to me of the matter. I must applaud you, Miss Elena. By not giving into pressure, your actions led to me catching a defector to his majesty's army. Of course, I know that is little consolation for how terribly he mistreated you, but hopefully it shall give you some comfort."

"Then your actions led to good ends," Kitty said to Elena, taking Elena's hand. "And you helped the army by it."

"It is not a small amount of comfort that I receive, I assure you," Elena said. "Indeed, I feel a little better. But poor Colonel— to know that you had such a man in your regiment. I am sorry."

"It is no reflection on me, fortunately. We Colonels are never responsible for our soldiers' romantic adventures. But we are responsible for administering punishment, and to that, I will uphold my duty. I was not told of the identity of the woman that he mistreated, but I didn't care for her name. The fact that Mr. Wilson was a disgusting fortune-hunter was enough for me to seek a reckoning. But fortunately, him being a deserter does lead to him being pressed under the weight of the law."

"What do you mean?" Georgiana asked.

"He deserted my regiment to run away and elope. When I received the news that he was found here, I came down here immediately to do my duty. After Mr. Wilson will give his deposition, he will be... I am afraid to say it, because I worry that it will be too much for your delicacy. But then, you are all very different sort of women. He will be flogged for his misconduct."

"Oh dear!" Jane professed, covering her mouth.

"Well," Kitty said, "this same thing happened in Meryton, actually. There was an officer who was flogged. And it is best that he will be punished for it."

"I can see what you mean," Georgiana added. "For if he were given no corporal punishment, then perhaps he would never learn his lesson. Also, it would lead to a bad example. If he was not punished, then other officers could think that they had the right to defect and be mercenary all that they wish."

"In such a circumstance," I finalized, "it could be argued that his pain at present will prevent him from causing more pain in the future."

"And even if I did not administer logic to this," Elena said at the end of our opinions, "I admit that I cannot feel any sympathy for him right now. I am not afraid of being mocked for lacking female delicacy, but no woman should remain delicate her entire life. Besides, delicacy is a talent that I never learned. So, no, I cannot sit here and weep for him, or feel sorry for his punishment. Rather... I feel as if he deserves it."

"No one will judge you," Mr. Darcy said, "for he has brought his fate upon himself."

At last, Colonel Fitzwilliam turned to Jane.

"I know that this news is alarming for you to hear it," he said, "but this is my duty, Miss Bennet. If I do not do it, then my duty will not have been done, the officer will never learn, and I display a lack of chivalry for not chastising a man who showed no feeling for a woman's heart."

Jane looked down.

"You mistook my exclamation, Colonel. I was just alarmed because of the image of the punishment. Yet, your duty is important. So was his sense of loyalty, but he lacked it. Therefore, honor must be upheld. Therefore, I understand. I will not gasp again."

"Thank you. Your kindness is still one of your greatest qualities."

As we ate on, Elena was silent for a time, but she had clearly been deliberating something.

"Colonel?" Elena asked.

"Yes?"

"I was wondering. When Mr. Wilson gives his deposition, can I be there to witness it?"

"It is highly unorthodox, and it is not permitted."

"Please, sir. This man promised me his heart and stole mine in the process. For a brief moment, I thought that I was escaping a terrible family. I thought that I was finally given a real chance in life. When his deception was unveiled, I felt that I had been blinded. And in that moment, I felt all chances fade. And that all possibilities of love and happiness would never be obtained. This will be my chance to confront this horrible situation and put it behind me."

"I thought that you would never wish to see him again," Georgiana acknowledged.

"On the contrary, I feel as if I will never be fully at peace until I do."

"Elena," Mr. Darcy said, "is there anything I can do to persuade you that this course of action is unwise?"

"No, there is nothing."

"Well then… Richard, is it possible that she can witness the deposition? I will escort her there."

Colonel Fitzwilliam leaned back in his chair.

"I don't know."

"If anyone has the right, Colonel," Kitty pressed, "Miss Elena does. Of course, the army only recognizes the offense that he committed against itself, but he committed a greater crime against her."

"Would it help if we talked to Colonel Forster?" Jane asked. "He would perhaps be more convinced, due to his desire to make his wife happy. He is always considerate of her, and he would feel guilty for not being chivalrous by denying Miss Elena."

"You all make it so hard to refuse," Colonel Fitzwilliam noted. "That is the one drawback with family. But of course, you are quite right. I will speak with Colonel Forster, and if he refuses, then yes, you all can appeal to him."

Elena gave him a grateful smile.

"Thank you, Colonel. This means a great deal to me."

Once more, Colonel Fitzwilliam stole another glance at Jane and then we continued speaking of the diversions in Brighton.

When we finished, we decided to walk along the streets of Brighton. The sun was setting, and yet, there was still the beauty of seeing the shore amidst the twilight hour.

We set out in the brisk evening air, and Colonel Fitzwilliam moved up ahead, with Jane, Kitty, Georgiana and Elena alongside him. He had Jane on one arm and Georgiana on the other, while Kitty and Elena were arm in arm.

Mr. Darcy and I distinctly lagged behind, with our arms also linked.

"Your cousin has four women to entertain," I noted.

"If anyone can achieve that, it's Richard," Darcy pointed out.

"True. When setting your minds to it, you and he have the remarkable ability to be very captivating."

"When have I ever been captivating?" His face relaxed even more.

"Even when I was uncivil to you, I could not keep you off my thoughts for more than half a day. It was very vexing how much your impressions rested in my mind."

"I had no idea of them doing so, but the feeling was mutual, as you know. I did everything to keep you from always being on my mind, but you kept rising to the surface of my thoughts anyhow."

"How tedious it must have been for you."

"Oh, very," he answered. "Also, I must inform you that there is a new development."

"There is always a new development. We are two of the few people in England who never have the chance to get bored."

"Which is even more ironic for me, because I am quite a dull sort of creature."

"You made the mistake of marrying a woman with four sisters, and then taking in the sister-who-never-was. Your life will never be the same again. So, what has happened now?"

"After Jane had me send the letters to Bingley and Richard, both men proved to be worth being called gentlemen, because they were. It was Mr. Bingley who wrote to Colonel Fitzwilliam first. Both men agreed to meet and talk about their dilemma. They both agreed to *never* press their attention on Jane, and if she chooses one of them, it is not of their influence. Also, they both promised each other that they both would be civil to one another, never hold the other in disdain, and always rise above jealousy or resentment."

"I should not be surprised, because I know they are good men. But I still am. They have dealt with it very well. I am happy for this."

I looked ahead at Jane as she said something to the Colonel.

"I marvel at her ability to be comfortable around him. They behave as if nothing happened."

"We behave that way whenever we argue. We have contradicted each other, questioned each other, and then we still united afterwards. Remember how you didn't dance with me at Lucas Lodge, then when you stayed at Netherfield Park, your mother attacked me, and you tried to defend me?"

"I did do that, didn't I?" I asked. "I wonder what I was thinking."

"I do not think you were thinking. Just like I wasn't thinking when I told Miss Bingley that I admired the sparkle that your three mile walk to Netherfield gave to your eyes. I think we both were instinctively trying to protect the other, despite our conflict with each other. Perhaps Jane is more like you than you think."

"I never would have known. Truly, I must stop thinking that I know everything about everyone. For there shall always be outliers." Suddenly, another thought came to me. "But wait! Do you think that Mr. Bingley knows about Colonel Fitzwilliam being here?"

"He does," Darcy informed me. "The Colonel wrote a letter to him, telling him about his duties here in Brighton. Bingley knows. The only thing that is called to question is what this will lead to Bingley doing?"

This news gave me relief. Whatever Bingley's course of action after this, at least he was not left in ignorance.

"Maybe you should write to him," I suggested, "he might want someone to talk to about what he's feeling."

"Ah, us men and our feelings. No one ever wants to hear about that."

"And maybe that's the problem," I extrapolated.

When I uttered the last sentence, Darcy turned to me.

"What I mean is," I elaborated, "is that you men, like us women sometimes, are not allowed to talk about what you are feeling. Because it is not proper. Sometimes, what *is* right is *not* proper. After all, look at us. We are not proper, but we feel right. And we are. What I am saying is… Mr. Darcy, sometimes, because of your strength, your power, your prestige and your stoicism, I can forget that you are human. And that you have as much a right to have feelings, and talk about those feelings, as much as you need to."

Mr. Darcy opened his mouth and closed it.

"What did that expression mean?" I asked.

"Forgive me, but it reminded me of my past for a moment."

"In what way?"

"You reminded me of my mother. She was the last person in my life who ever let me talk about my feelings."

"When did your mother pass away?"

"Six years ago."

"It's been that long since anyone asked you about your emotions?" I asked, surprised.

"Yes. I suppose that is why the relationship between a mother and a son is one of the most important in a man's life. They see us grow from infancy, and were there when we were sad, when we cut and scraped our knee, when we hurt ourselves, when we were afraid, when we felt insecure, when we suffered under our own failures and bad behavior, and when we have nightmares of our past mistakes coming back to haunt us. They were often there when we were crying in the middle of the night and we needed someone to tell us that no monsters were coming for us out of the darkness. When a mother sees her son, she sees all the emotions that she must nurture, encourage, and protect. When other people see us, we are told not to have emotions. So, after she died, there seemed to be no room for me being frail. There was no room for me to talk about my deepest desires, my worries, and my fears. We men can't be afraid, can't cry, can't fall, and cannot question why we have no right to fall sometimes. To everyone, I was just a great stone that they had to lean on for support. But what was I to lean on? Where was I to go?"

I tapped my hand against his, offering him solace.

"You have me. This is where you always can go, and you can always be. Of course, I know that I can never fully replace the strength of a mother's love. But I will always be here for you. You can lose all your wealth, your home, and your prestige in life, but I will still be here. Even after all your beauty has faded—for fade it will."

He looked down on me.

"Elizabeth, I am so scared sometimes."

This confession was so raw, so real, and it laid his soul completely bare. In this moment, I had to tread lightly, because Mr. Darcy was fragile. He was right. There was no room for fragility amongst men of our times. Either you were strong, or you were weak. There was no in-between.

"I am proud of you," I encouraged. "It takes great courage to admit one's fears. You are braver now than you have ever been. I had no idea that could be even more lovely." Raising on my toes, I kissed him. "When we first met, why didn't you tell me that I was in love with you?"

He chuckled.

"I thought it would be more amusing for you to figure it out on your own."

"But I must ask, now that you are willing to confess your feelings, were you hurt when I saw Mr. Wickham? Did seeing me talk with him arouse any insecurities that you felt? Regarding the fact that I once preferred his company."

He looked ahead, his eyes turning to stone again.

"No," I insisted, "we shall have none of that. I am here to listen, and there is nothing to be ashamed of. If you tell me how you felt, then I can help. And you will find peace."

"I am afraid to talk," he admitted. "For it is unwise."

"Why is it unwise?"

"Because my feelings are irrational."

"Feelings are not often born out of sense, but usually out of sensibility. Emotions are not always going to be logical. But if you never tell me what you feel, then it might grow in you, and I do not ever want you to turn away from me in resentment."

"Very well..." he breathed in heavily and continued. "Elizabeth, no matter what I say now, please remember that I am very much in love with you. The passionate attachment that I feel is so deep, that it can never be undone."

"I will remember."

"I know that your preference for Mr. Wickham's company sprang from him being charming and flattering you. He also offered you a connection that I did not offer. Therefore, free of any ties to me, mingled with the fact that I gave you nothing in return, and never told you the truth about Wickham's behavior, leaving you unprotected from his deception, your actions were natural— and you may even argue that it's my fault that you and Mr. Wickham became close. If I had acted on my affection for you earlier, then he never would have succeeded. I know ALL of this. And yet... I am still angry with you."

"Why?" I asked, remaining calm and refusing to be rash.

"Because you liked him before you ever liked me. I try and remind myself that this should not affect me. But it does. I have no right to be affected, but it hurts that you favored him so much, while you held me in contempt. It is not logical, but it is how I feel. Do you despise me?"

"No," I assured him. "I hated how warmly I thought of Wickham when you told me the truth. I felt as if I injured you. But I never knew how deep the wound went. Now, please remember two things. First, I *was never* in love with Mr. Wickham. I favored him, was flattered by his attentions, but it was never love.

But I am in love with you, and I would have been from the beginning if you had given me a reason to do so. And that is the second thing that you must remember. Like you said, your influence shaped my friendship with him. Therefore, we both are to blame for this."

"I know, and I keep telling myself that."

"But seeing me speak with him revived your fears of my preference to him."

"Yes."

"This attitude of yours perhaps is natural, even though it is not something that you need to worry about. Since it is natural, it is never going to die. You are always going to be a little upset about this. Whenever you do, come and tell me about it, and I will always do my best to remind you that I will always love you, and I never loved him. Together, we can help you rise above this agony."

"Thank you," he said. "Always help me, Lizzy."

"I will, Fitzwilliam."

We walked on, until it got so late that it was time to return to the hotel with the others.

# CHAPTER 11

## FAMILY TRIALS

*T*he next day, I got a letter from Rosings Park.

"It's from Charlotte," I told Jane as we sat in our room. "I didn't even know that she was aware that I was staying here."

Suddenly, I lowered the letter in shock.

"Lizzy, what is it?"

"That's just it! She would only know of my being here if Lady Catherine mentioned it."

"Well, naturally."

"Jane, Lady Catherine wanted Darcy to marry her daughter, Anne de Bourgh."

Jane's eyes widened.

"Oh!"

Looking at the letter, I held it with trepidation.

"And I have the suspicion that this letter is not just written to wish me good fortune."

Sitting down, I opened the missive and began to read it.

*Dear Elizabeth,*

*I have heard news of your engagement to Mr. Darcy, and I confess that I am so glad of your good fortune. First, you deserve such a fate and I am happy that your family now shall be secure. Your cares are over, and the ladies of Longbourn will now have a home. This now makes my heart happy, and for the first time since your poor father passed away, you can find security in your future.*

*Second, I find particular joy in this for selfish reasons. I am happy to see just how right I was! Elizabeth, mark all the times that I believed that Mr. Darcy was in love with you, and you refused to listen. Now you can determine, for yourself, just how accurate I was. As self-indulgent as this is to admit, but it is always so gratifying to one's pride by knowing that one can occasionally be correct. For I did not see what I wanted to see; I saw what was really there.*

*Now that I have expressed my wishes, I can tell you my warning.*

*I have your address and know of where you are, because Lady Catherine knows. Just like she knows that you are engaged to her nephew, the very man who she intended for her daughter. Elizabeth, to say that she does not look on your engagement with a friendly eye would be me putting it mildly. Lady Catherine is enraged. And I believe that her resentment shall go further than simply her writing a bitter letter to you both. I believe that she is intending to see her point through, and you know that she has no fear in talking. I have not been taken into her confidence at the moment, and nor has Anne. Therefore, I am warning you and Mr. Darcy. I think she is coming to you. But I do not know for certain.*

*Other than that, my present circumstance is everything that I have hoped for. You are aware that I never held marriage high in regard, and only committed to it because it was my duty and the only means through which a gentleman's daughter can do.*

*But I still have my autonomy in one way: I am not a burden at home. I care for that a great deal. Also, Anne is not quite as shut up as she used to be. Her constitution is still weak, but the new reverend to Hunsford, a Mr. Orwell, has proven to be a very valuable asset to our company. He is not married to Lady Catherine's pleasure and displeasure. She insists that he must marry, but she also revels in the idea of choosing his bride for him.*

*After all, Lady Catherine prides herself on her excellent judgment. Often, Mr. Orwell must call at Rosings for more than just to report his sermons, living habits and food consumption, but he has proven to be a very good conversationalist. Anne and he seem to have developed a friendly relationship, and he calls just to speak to us sometimes. Around him, Anne has life and vitality, because she is given time to talk and form her own thoughts. If there is one thing that benefited from my poor husband's demise, it is that Mr. Orwell has taken his place well. He delivers good sermons, he is steady and is a man of information, and Anne is improving under him.*

*Together, she and I have gone to the church and helped him decorate it during special services. I want to believe that I am a good companion for her. Therefore, my life is full and complete.*

*Yet, for my warning, mark my words… prepare yourself.*

*Yours etc.*
*Charlotte*

Lowering the letter, I sighed.

"Jane, Lady Catherine knows, and she knows where we are. I must brace myself."

"Surely, she would prefer her nephew's happiness more than her own schemes."

I gave her a shrewd look.

"But then," Jane furthered, "you do know her better than I do."

"Oh, I know her well," I remarked, rolling my eyes as I headed for the door. "Now, I must share this 'happy' news."

Leaving our room, I knocked on Mr. Darcy's door.

When he opened it, he had a letter in his hand.

"I came to tell you," I said, "your aunt knows where we are, and I do not think she is happy."

He raised up the letter in his hand.

"Oh, I know she is not."

Darcy gave me the letter, which his aunt sent, and it was everything that could be expected. She scolded, threatened, and implored him to write back to tell her that our engagement was a false rumor. She also said some unpleasing things about my character. When I finished reading, I handed the letter back to him.

"Yes, she knows indeed," I said, "though, I will be a little amused when I imagine what her face will look like when you tell her that the rumor is not false."

"Yes," Mr. Darcy said, "that would be a sight. Well, there is nothing for it."

"Yes, you must write back, for this is a bridge that we must cross."

He placed his hand on my cheek.

"Remember, all she has are her words. And they carry very little weight when it comes to my heart. At Pemberley, she can never reach us."

"At Pemberley, we will be safe. Write that letter, dear Mr. Darcy. Let us face the wave that is her dissatisfaction. For when we overcome that, I believe that we can overcome anything."

Mr. Darcy wrote the letter and sent it. A storm was coming, but it would come another day.

---

Colonel Fitzwilliam came to us again that day, giving us the successful news that Colonel Forster granted permission for Elena and Mr. Darcy to attend Mr. Wilson's deposition. This acceptance did not surprise me. For I knew that Colonel Forster was a kind man who understood this sort of need.

Since it was a fine day, we all went out onto the Grand Brighton's legendary Victoria Terrace, had their legendary tea, and then Elena escorted us around the town square. Kitty saw a gown that she liked in a shop window. She requested that Elena and the rest of us should take her there again one day, so that she could purchase it. She did not wish to bore the men by making them shop with her. This was readily agreed to, and eventually, we found a lovely dining hall to eat in, where we tasted the delights that Brighton had to offer.

Afterwards, we returned to the hotel to prepare ourselves for the next day.

"How are you feeling?" Georgiana asked Elena. "You must be worried about seeing Mr. Wilson tomorrow."

"On the contrary," Elena said, "I look forward to it. I want to look into the eyes of the man who deceived me. It is strange, I know, but I refuse to be alarmed."

"That is very good," Colonel Fitzwilliam said. "I believe that you have much to your reward. For, I saw him briefly before I came to visit you all, and he appeared very penitent. Then again, he could have simply been acting. Or merely sad that he was caught, rather than sad because he feels how wrong he is."

"Perhaps we shall never know," Kitty pointed out. "But I suppose that this is all that can be hoped for. Especially since none of us can change the past."

"True."

"I do not want to change the past," Elena said, "as strange as it is, but I like where I am now."

We were all happy about this.

Before all of us women retired, I managed to get a moment alone with Mr. Darcy. He and the Colonel were going to spend a little longer together in the billiards room. And my next comment was a selfish one.

"Darcy," I whispered, "I know that this is wrong of me, but I must ask. Do you think you could ask the Colonel if I might attend the deposition with you all as well? Of course, I am not the woman he slighted, but this still affects our family. I want to go with you. Also, it would be good for Elena to have another woman with her."

"I was wondering if you secretly wished to go. I suspected that you might. I'll ask him. If Colonel Forster has agreed to have Elena go, then I cannot see why he would be upset about your coming. I believe that he will agree, and he can tell the Colonel about your addition when he goes back to Old Ship Hotel."

"Thank you." I kissed him lightly on the cheek.

Going back to my room, I felt lighter. I would have spent a large portion of the next day curious about what Mr. Wilson would have said and done. Now I didn't have to hear it secondhand. I could witness it.

After Mr. Darcy and I had opened up to each other, I felt like now I could ask him anything and there would be no barriers between us.

Naturally, arguments and disagreement will ensue. That is never the problem with marriage, for both partners cannot always be one in agreement. Yet, I believed that we would still be one, even if we disagreed. For now we would always talk.

# CHAPTER 12

## THE INTERROGATION

The next day, I dressed with care as I joined Mr. Darcy and Elena. We met Colonel Fitzwilliam at the Old Ship Hotel, who informed us that Mr. Wilson was being detained at the camp.

Colonel Forster had shown no signs of objecting to my attendance, due to the wisdom of having another woman present with Elena.

We all proceeded to the militia's camp and we entered the headquarters where Elena's past love was imprisoned. We sat in a small chamber, while there were two chairs and tables in the middle of the room. Colonel Fitzwilliam sat on one chair while an officer was brought into the room. He was shackled, his uniform was dirty, his face hadn't been washed recently and his hair was not combed. The man was not ugly, nor was he handsome. His looks were comfortable and no more. That being said, he perhaps was the sort of man whose beauty rested in his manners. Charisma is often more charming than perfect features.

Upon entering, he first beheld Colonel Fitzwilliam, and then his eyes moved past him, finally resting on Elena. When seeing her, he stopped, blinked in shock, opened his mouth as if he was about to say something, but then closed it upon reconsideration.

"Take a seat, Mr. Wilson," Colonel Fitzwilliam invited.

Still with his hands shackled, James Wilson walked up to the chair, sat down, and placed his hands on the table. Colonel Fitzwilliam removed some paper from his satchel bag, as well as a pen and some ink, then he began to read off the paper. Of course, we were not alone. There were four other officers in the room, and they stood in the four corners of the walls.

"How are you feeling?" I whispered to Elena, worried about her.

"I am not affected, I assure you," Elena whispered in reply.

"State your name for the deposition," Colonel Fitzwilliam said.

"James Aaron Wilson," Mr. Wilson said. "Age 30, born in Yorkshire. To parents Mr. Harold Wilson and Miss Henrietta Darby."

Colonel Fitzwilliam leaned back, analyzing the man.

"You give me all your information before asking. I cannot tell if you are wishing to cooperate now, or because you have experience with this sort of situation."

"I do it simply because I do not wish to cause any trouble."

"And by that, you mean that you do not wish to cause any more trouble than you already have."

"I am sorry for what I have done," Mr. Wilson urged. "You must believe me."

"You were running away to get married?"

"Yes."

"Funny, because if you had informed your commanding officer about this, which was me, then I would have given you leave to perform your nuptials. Getting married does not take much time to do. A man can be engaged, wed, and back to his duties in a week."

"I was a man in love."

"You were a man who was mercenary, and the reason that you ran away was because you were aware that the woman you chose was wealthy, you were not, and her parents would never have approved."

"Precisely," he urged, "as you say, I am poor, and no one ever cares about love when one's pocketbook is empty."

"So, you are going to pretend that your actions were not mercenary, despite that evidence has been brought forward to determine that you were marrying a woman primarily for her dowry. Because I have proof of the reverse." Colonel Fitzwilliam turned directly to Miss Elena.

"This deposition will now recognize a key witness, this woman, who was the woman that this libertine tried to elope with."

All the officers turned to Elena.

"And all present will not ever mention her presence here at all," Colonel Fitzwilliam said to the officers. "Is that understood?"

All the men agreed.

"Now," Colonel Fitzwilliam continued, "Madame, is it true that Mr. Wilson here planned to elope with you?"

"It is," Elena said.

"And is it true that the only reason he was not successful was because you overheard and saw a letter indicating how he would now come into money, because of the dowry that he was marrying."

"Yes, I did," Elena said again, then she turned to Mr. Wilson. "Are you going to deny it, James? Are you going to accuse me of being a liar after all the other ways that you hurt me?"

Mr. Wilson looked down at the desk.

"Are you going to still cling to innocence long after you have lost that quality?" Elena furthered. "Are you? Speak up, damn you!"

This vulgar phrasing made everyone in the room flinch. Elena was a gentleman's daughter from her head to her feet. To see so refined a woman resort to such base words was enough to make all of us see the gravity of the situation. We all looked down, terrified under the weight of her feelings. We felt like we were witnessing something that we didn't have the right to.

"Go on, James," Elena continued, her voice softer, but no less bold, "say something unnatural."

"Miss—"

"Do not use her name," Colonel Fitzwilliam overrode. "You may be named in your villainy, but let her go nameless in her victimhood."

Wilson breathed in and continued.

"Madam," he said to Elena, "I promise you, that the situation was more complicated than what I might have given you the impression of."

"It is simple, sir. You wanted my money."

"I do not deny that your income was another aspect that added to your charms. I see that there is no point in denying it. But I did admire you and I found you very agreeable."

"But you never mention love, Mr. Wilson. And that is obvious."

"Due to my circumstances at home when growing up, I have learned to be frightened of the idea of love. I only understand companionship. That is what I looked for in a wife."

"And that, Mr. Wilson, was you saying something unnatural. Friendship can be found anywhere, but the bond between a husband and wife ought to be something more special. Colonel Fitzwilliam, my apologies for interrupting your interrogation. Please, continue."

"Thank you," Colonel Fitzwilliam said, writing down more observations in his report. "So, sir, now your character has been made apparent."

"I know what I must appear as," Mr. Wilson continued, "but sir, if you and all here would know me better, I promise that it is more complicated."

"You are in my regiment, James. I am your commanding officer. You really do not think I know you?"

"I beg your pardon, Colonel, I didn't mean to offend. It is just that we have never spoken, so I know that you do not know my situation."

Now, the Colonel could continue his interrogation.

Colonel Fitzwilliam placed his pen on the paper and leaned back in his chair with a steely gaze.

"Your name *is* James Aaron Wilson, you *are* 30, and you *were* raised in Yorkshire. Your closest friends in my regiment are officers Oliver Davison and Frederick Thornton. You were Fred's best man when he married. You like fishing, you are an adept swimmer, and you favor your left leg, because your right leg has a little less feeling in it."

Mr. Wilson blinked, surprised by this.

"You disarm me, sir," Mr. Wilson admitted.

"Naturally," Colonel Fitzwilliam stated. "You see, I am your commanding officer, not your friend. That puts me in a tight space of being unable to become your friend, or else I will not be able to be objective in performing my duties. I wish that I could be your friend, but I do not know how to establish that proper balance between camaraderie and discipline. I do not know how to be strict with my comrades. But that never stops me from observing everything around me, including my officers. Your feelings of being obscure never rendered you invisible. I always saw you, Mr. Wilson."

"Oh," Mr. Wilson said, "I am honored that you know about me then. When it comes to my past superiors, this makes you better."

"Ah, so you are driven by a need to feel special and loved?"

"Have you ever met a man or woman who doesn't want that?"

Colonel Fitzwilliam raised an eyebrow at this.

"Fair point, but it matters how a man goes about trying to obtain it. That is what differentiates real men from rakes."

"If I waited till I was good enough for women, I would never have one."

"That is not my problem."

"But, sir, please understand that I mean no offense, for you are right, that this is *not* your problem. But it is mine. And I tire of it being mine. I do not want to waste my life, never having the means to have a comfortable family life and… to have a family." Here, Mr. Wilson looked at Elena. Then he turned back to Colonel Fitzwilliam. "I know that this makes no difference, but I am happy that you know me a little better now."

"Actually," the Colonel continued, taking some files out of his satchel. "I know you more than you think. You see, while my other officers are always happy for their fellow redcoats when they marry, not *all* of them are very sympathetic to men who elope for mercenary means. So, they had no problem in—what is the best word for it—oh yes: blab. A few of them told me about how they realized your deception and kept your promise, until now." He dropped some papers in front of Mr. Wilson. "Like how your name is not even James Wilson."

Mr. Wilson's eyes widened in shock.

"Sir," Colonel Fitzwilliam declared, "who is the stranger who is sitting in front of me?"

This announcement made all of us sit up straighter in our seats. It was as if we had been hit by a bolt of lightning. Instinctively, I turned to Elena, who I saw look alarmed for the first time since we met. She was a woman who was so light and confident, that nothing seemed to affect her. But now she looked shaken.

Her expression was nothing compared to Mr. Wilson's face. He had turned pale white.

"I can see that you know that there is no point in denying it," Colonel Fitzwilliam stated, "so, I will give you one chance to tell us your real name."

"Colonel," Mr. Wilson sighed, "what is really in a name?"

"Do not bring Shakespeare into this. If you do that, I will be tempted to take my rapier and run it through your chest."

What if Jane saw the Colonel now! I found his strength to be very impressive and fascinating. Jane might have been a little apprehensive about it at first, but I believed that eventually she would be proud of the Colonel.

"Now," Colonel Fitzwilliam pressed. "What is your name?!"

"Joseph," Mr. Wilson said. "Joseph Martin."

"There now, I believe that is the first honest thing that you have said. And since you can tell that I knew that already, then naturally you are aware that I know a significant portion of your story. For what is the reason that you favor your left leg and that you had to bury your name in obscurity? It is because you used to be a sailor in his majesty's navy. And you defected from that. You have been a deserter twice!"

This second offense made Elena cover her face with her hands. Truly, this must have been so painful for her.

Desperate, Mr. Wilson—or Mr. Martin—leaned forward.

"This is where the root of my trouble all begins," he insisted. "Madam and Colonel, you do not understand. I favor my left leg, because my right leg was wounded, but not from battle. I served under a Captain Thomas Morgan, who clearly got his position from being of noble birth. He was insane. He would beat us and practically torture us sailors when we were out at sea. Everything that we did was wrong. The reason that I have lost a lot of life in my right leg is because he beat it and stomped on it because I accidentally dropped a candle on the floor, and it left a burn mark. Everyone, please believe me, he was a monster. When we made berth back in Portsmouth, I knew that I would be arrested if I got caught, but I didn't care. This was my one chance at finding freedom. No one ever talks about those of us who are born low and our fight to survive the world who will never regard us as equal. And then we are blamed for trying to have a better life."

"Wanting a better life is always natural," Elena interrupted. "I understand this better than anyone. First, I do not even know if you are telling me the truth. You lied about your name, so now you could have been lying about everything! Either way, what is the point of it if you are going to be as malicious as the people you tried to escape? They abused you, and so you use that as an excuse to take advantage of me? Who gains now?"

"Who indeed?" Colonel Fitzwilliam supported. "So, you deserted, and that was the last time that anyone ever heard of Joseph Martin."

"I let that name go, named myself James Wilson, enlisted in the army and no one asked any more questions. When enlisting, the army is more concerned with having soldiers than they are with your history. And I started my new life."

"And the Captain is the only reason that you are not flogged already," Colonel Fitzwilliam enlightened him. "You see, Joseph Martin never actually disappeared. You had been recognized by a few soldiers and sailors who knew who you really were. They just didn't care, because they also knew that you served under Captain Morgan, whose insanity and brutality eventually became evident to his superiors. Not only was he stricken from his position, but he has been dishonorably discharged."

Mr. Martin leaned forward, his shackles clanging against the desk.

"What?!" He gasped.

"Yes. I cannot deny that you are telling me the truth now, because the truth became soon known. If I can date your desertion at the right month, you sadly might have had better fortune if you had waited. Perhaps no more than a month after you ran, Captain Morgan was discharged and is never allowed in the navy again."

Mr. Martin covered his face, frustrated.

"If only I had waited a month."

"Yes. In that manner, I am sorry for you. Most likely, you did not deserve to be maimed, or the treatment that you suffered. Of that, I am happy that you escaped that situation. And if you had lived out your life, doing your duty in the militia, you would have remained in obscurity, never found again. Your present defection will not be alleviated, because it was not the result of being abused. Rather, it was the result of avarice. Therefore, do you plead guilty for your actions?"

"I do."

"You shall be flogged fifteen times, and then imprisoned for a month, before you are stationed at another post. I cannot have you return to mine, because that would give the other officers a bad example. Do you understand these terms?"

"Yes." Mr. Martin closed his eyes.

"The one and only thing that I can give you now, is your name. Since Mr. Joseph Martin will never be condemned for deserting Captain Morgan's ship, his name is innocent. Therefore, you can return to being Joseph Martin once more."

"That… that is more than I hoped."

"See?" Colonel Fitzwilliam said, putting the paper in front of him. "A name can mean much. Now I shall ask you to sign this."

Mr. Martin signed the document and sighed.

"At least now I can stop running."

"Yes."

The deposition was finished, and Colonel Fitzwilliam closed the folder.

"Now, do you have anything else that you want to say to me, or anyone else that is present?"

"Yes, I do."

Mr. Martin breathed in and he turned to Elena.

"Madam," he began, "I know that no excuse that I give can ever be remedied, but, whatever my past actions and my present course, please believe that I did find you very agreeable, and I did feel a strong sort of attachment."

"But not love," Elena continued, then she stood up. "Taking your history into consideration, I understand why you abandoned your past profession, and why you let your real name pass off into obscurity, for it was out of a desperate desire to survive. I am sorry for how you were treated, for no one deserves such abuse. But nor do I deserve it as well. For here is what makes this all so terribly pathetic; you were going to hand me over to such a fate. I cannot be blind that you saw me as your chance to escape your past even more." She briefly put her hand over her mouth.

"If you married me, then you would have my dowry and would inherit my family's home. You could abandon any profession altogether and had become a gentleman and would be above any reproach. This could have been forgiven if you had just been honest with me from the very beginning. If once we developed an attachment, you had revealed your real life and identity to me, and then gave me the option of if I still wished to choose you. But you did not. You neither trusted me, nor confided in me, or respected me. Just because you have been abused in your past does not give you the right to abuse me in the present. I don't care for such hypocrisy. And you lied to your Colonel. You lied to so many, many of whom could have helped you. If you had married me, then this propensity for deception could have continued. You could have spent our marriage lying to me, and never feeling for me more than a friend. You would have doomed me to a cursed life. I would have been married to a man who gave me a false name! So, our union would have been false as well. I am happy that you escaped such a hostile environment, but no, Mr. Martin. It shall be a long time before I ever wish to face you again. Yet, I wish you good luck, good fortune, and to be a better man than the man I knew."

Elena nodded to us and we all stood up. As we did, I didn't notice that my reticule was no longer wrapped around my wrist, but it had sunk to the floor. Elena noticed this.

"Miss Bennet," she spoke without thinking, "your reticule."

She picked it up and handed it to me.

"Thank you," I said, and then we noticed that Mr. Martin was eyeing us very intently. He knew my name now!

"Bennet?" Mr. Martin repeated. "Your name is Miss Bennet?"

"Yes," I answered.

"Her identity is no concern of yours," Mr. Darcy demanded.

"Yes, forgive me," Mr. Martin rushed out, "but I must ask. Are you related to Miss Lydia Bennet?"

"Yes, I am. She is my younger sister. Why do you ask?"

"I am sorry. Perhaps it is nothing."

His questions were curious to me, but I knew that it was not my place to ask.

Therefore, Mr. Darcy, Elena and I left, overhearing Colonel Fitzwilliam order the soldiers to not utter a word of us being there at the proceedings.

---

Walking back to the Grand Brighton, I looked at Elena.

"How are you feeling?" I asked her.

"The answer may be unwise."

"What is important is never unwise."

"True. I am embarrassed, heartbroken, and feel so unwanted. His history has softened me toward his situation, for he deserved better than how he was treated, but it is not my fault that he was born poor! It is no rich person's fault when anyone is born poor, just as it is wrong when people are punished for not being rich. He may have been kind, and he may have been a kind husband, but he may have never loved me. The feeling of being unloved by the man that you choose makes a woman feel so ugly. He almost robbed me of my confidence. If he had only told the truth, all could have been different. But it wasn't. So, here I am."

"I know a little bit about being attended to because of one's wealth," Mr. Darcy said. "I know that is not a pleasant experience. You are being regarded for your pocketbook, while you have to be suspicious of those because of their lack of one."

"And what do you do when you wake up from that revelation?" Elena asked. "When you realize that you are your money, and you always will be."

"I recall that there is nothing to actually fear. It matters not how others view me, but how I view myself. I am aware of my self-worth and I will not let anything destroy that. Do not let this experience shake your fortitude. No one is worth that in the end."

"You are correct, cousin. I just wish that my heart would listen."

"My fiancé is correct in his advice," I supported, "but do not hate yourself for not being able to rein your heart in just yet. It needs time to recover, and when it does, you shall be as you once were. We have all been fools when it comes to love, in one way or another. Be happy, Elena, you landed on your feet."

# CHAPTER 13

## BEFORE THE STORM SET IN

Since part of the day was over, we could not spend it visiting historical sites, and the Colonel would be most occupied. Rather, Mr. Darcy suggested that we return to the town square and inquire at the dress shop, to see if we wanted any new gowns.

"Dearest," I said, "you do not need to trouble yourself on our account. For going to the dressmaker's is something that will be great fun for us, but you would be miserable."

"Not particularly," Mr. Darcy said, "as long as I have the right to sit in a corner, given refreshments and allowed to read the gazette, I will be just as happy there as I am here. I will not feel imposed upon. Besides," and here, he looked a little bashful, "this also might be a good chance for you to choose your wedding gown, and for your sisters to choose their bridesmaids dresses."

"And you blush when you ask this." Kitty chuckled, nudging Georgiana with her elbow. "I think you look charming right now."

"I suppose that I might have felt uncomfortable with being so forward."

"Well, you passed it off splendidly," I assured him.

"But what of Elena," Kitty said, taking Elena's arm in hers. "She is family now."

"Yes, she is," I agreed. "Elena, if you can get a gown as well that would be a similar color to my sisters, I would like it if you were a part of the wedding party."

"I shall be delighted," Elena agreed, "if my other cousin finds the idea agreeable."

"I do," Mr. Darcy confirmed. "Now, let us all go to the town square and hope that they have a chair for me to sit on."

"And on the chair, you will see all of the world," I joked, kissing him on the cheek.

We left for the dress shop, and when we entered, the ladies saw to us immediately.

"When at home," Jane said to Mr. Darcy, "we often just wore the same gowns with different touches to them. But I do not believe that I have ever been in a shop like this."

"I can pay once sales are complete," Mr. Darcy said to the shop owner. "These four ladies require a similar gown of the same color and cloth that they choose, and my fiancée, Miss Elizabeth Bennet, requires a wedding gown. They shall also need two ballgowns, three dresses that are appropriate for visits, and a new coat and pair of gloves each."

"Mr. Darcy," I took his hands, merry. "That is all too exorbitant."

"Your words are saying that I should adhere to modesty, but your eyes display immense flattery."

"I cannot help but be a walking contradiction now. I do not want you to think that I shall be an expensive wife, but I also admire that you are willing to show such attention to us."

"Very well. Let me spoil you now, and then we shall practice economy when we marry."

"That is a bargain that I can willingly make."

"My chief request to you all though," he advised, "get gowns that suit your beauty, augment your loveliness, and flatters your figure. Some gowns can be so ostentatious that it renders the wearer looking uncomfortable, gaudy, and… just ugly."

We all laughed at this.

"I believe my future husband is encouraging us to be more like ourselves than anyone else," I elaborated. "I believe we can trust our own judgment."

With such a rich client who was willing to pay immediately, the women in the store all saw to us immediately and the attention was something we were unaccustomed to, so we became excited.

"I must explain our joy," Kitty said to Elena as we were all being measured, and cloth was presented to us. "We have not been accustomed to being the main one that shopkeepers tend to, so this is a delight."

"Getting new gowns shall never cease to be wonderful," Elena insisted, "so I share your excitement."

Mr. Darcy requested a chair, and two shop-boys brought him one immediately, along with a small table, some tea was brought to him, and he even got the newspaper that he wanted... for what little good that gave him!

No more than a few minutes after he began to read, some ready-made gowns were brought to us, and his curiosity was piqued.

Soon, we were ushered into dressing-rooms, where we each emerged once we finished to see how we looked in the mirrors. That was when Mr. Darcy first lowered his paper, then after the third woman emerged with her new gown on, he let the newspaper rest on the desk, and we had his undivided attention.

He seemed to revel in it all. Soon, he was asking us to twirl around so that he could see the entire gown, to ensure that it was worth the purchase. All of us were highly amused by it.

"Is it me," Jane asked him, "or do you understand muslin?"

"Of course, I do," Mr. Darcy chuckled as the shop woman brought him some cake. "My mother had the most beautiful gowns in the world, while also never falling into the sin of being gaudy. Her influence couldn't help but have some sort of lingering effect upon me."

When trying on my third gown, the other women were still in the rooms, changing, and I had Mr. Darcy's undivided attention. This latest gown was the best one that I had selected so far, and I hoped that he would like it. Upon seeing me, he stood up, walked up to me and he looked down at the gown.

"You will wear this one often?" he asked.

"It will make you happy," I noted. "And yes, I will wear it often."

"I love it."

"Then we have the wonderful prospect of being in agreement together. By the way, I want my wedding gown to be a peach color. Would you find that agreeable?"

"Yes. Peach will flatter you."

"I am happy that you like it. Since it does, I was thinking of the girls have a darker color of the same style. Like a burnt sienna color. We all will feel like we are part of one set."

"Yes. I agree."

"I hope I give you no reason to be ashamed."

"You will not."

We had meant to spend perhaps an hour there, but it turned into the remainder of the day. When we finished, we each had purchased four new gowns, gloves, a shawl, a few stockings and a custom cloak.

Mr. Darcy ordered that they be delivered to our hotel, and the shop owner was delighted at how much we had spent. Thanking Mr. Darcy repeatedly, she assured us that our wedding gowns would be ready for the first fitting in a week.

When we left the shop, our sisters and cousin were merrily speaking with each other, and Mr. Darcy and I were allowed to remain a little distance back.

"You were a delight," I said, warmly nudging his shoulder. "And to think that I felt so sorry that we would be making you suffer our company in a dress shop. But you embraced the situation."

"I found it not altogether tedious."

He was mincing his words, and I knew it.

"That is an understatement," I furthered, "come now, my beautiful friend. Admit it. You liked seeing us parade around in gowns the whole day. I think you gained some sort of satisfaction out of it."

"Oh, very well, it was… quite intoxicating."

"Oh, intoxicating is the word you put to it?" I asked, with an eyebrow raised.

"You all just kept coming out, looking lovelier and lovelier, that I was driven to distraction. We spent the morning watching a man be sentenced to being flogged, and you all literally made me forget that whole incident. I just felt drowned in beauty. As materialistic as that may sound, I could not help but happily fall into it. You all were so much like a pride of sirens and you called out to me. And that last gown made me fall to my knees. It makes me even wonder how I avoided falling in love with you for so long."

"Whatever crime that people label to being obsessed with beauty, I defy them now. You have every right to admire us in that way, and I liked it. Once more, we felt like a team."

Once more, we stopped at the dining hall where we would have our dinner, but as we did, we came upon four familiar faces.

"Miss Bennet!"

We turned and there was Mr. Bingley, with Mr. Hurst and his sisters, who had been the ones to call out. The Bingleys had come to Brighton.

# CHAPTER 14

## THE OTHER GOOD MAN

"*Miss* Bingley," Jane started, having to pretend to be enthusiastic for people that she could not have been more unhappy to see. "Mrs. And Mr. Hurst. And Mr. Bingley, you have come to Brighton."

"Yes, we have," Mrs. Hurst said. "And we see that there have been such friends to be met."

"This is quite the surprise," I remarked, secretly upset.

"And it is a pleasure to see you all again," Mr. Bingley said. "We all know each other, but I see a new face." Here, he looked at Elena.

"We all are acquainted, save one," Mr. Darcy said. "Allow me to introduce my cousin, Miss Elena Darcy."

Brief introductions were made between Elena and the Bingleys before Darcy questioned their arrival.

"Bingley," Mr. Darcy said, "I had not known that you were coming to Brighton."

"Yes," Mr. Bingley said, apprehensive, "forgive my lack of communication on that score. Faith, I had no intention of visiting Brighton at this time, but family is my excuse."

"And invitations as well," Miss Bingley added. "Sir Aleck Granger has recently come to Brighton to assist in the Dalton's new tradition of a Winter Brighton Ball."

"Sir Aleck is in Brighton?" Kitty asked, perking up. "Truly?"

"Yes," Miss Bingley said, her expression faltering when talking to Kitty. "Once more, he finds himself to be the center of party arrangements."

"He would be," Mr. Darcy stated. "Sir Aleck's talent at ball arrangements and guestlists are unparalleled. No one else knows how to plan something like he does. When not arranging his own parties, he is begged by everyone to arrange theirs."

"And we have been invited to come to Brighton," Mrs. Hurst said, "as Mr. Dalton's sister's most particular friends."

"And I was ordered very quickly to come," Mr. Bingley replied, "for my sisters successfully convinced me that I would slight the Daltons if I did not come as well."

"And you would have, Charles," Miss Bingley pressed. "When it comes to the Daltons, your company is implied, and you are at the time in your life when having friends is the greatest thing."

"And one can never have enough friends like the Daltons," Mr. Hurst said. "Darcy, I am surprised that you have not gotten an invitation."

"I am not," Mr. Darcy said, "for all that I am aware, perhaps the Daltons do not fancy my company."

"How could they not fancy your company?" Miss Bingley asked. "You are Mr. and Miss Darcy, after all!"

"Thank you, Miss Bingley," Mr. Darcy said, "but I must be realistic. I have been in Brighton for a couple of days, and I failed to inform many of our acquaintance that I was coming. Therefore, if any invitations are given, then they were sent to my house in town, and will take a little longer to be forwarded to me."

"Ah, that must have been it," Miss Bingley said. "Yes, that would account for it."

"Where are you all staying?" Mr. Bingley asked.

"The Grand Brighton Hotel," Mr. Darcy answered.

"That is where we are staying," Mrs. Hurst expressed. "That shall make our plans easy to make, for we have so much to acquaint you with."

"I am hungry," Mr. Hurst said, randomly. Mrs. Hurst rolled her eyes at him. "It is time to dine soon."

"It is," Miss Bingley acknowledged, then she turned to us. "Do you know any dining establishments that have the best merit?"

"We were going to dine now," Elena informed them, and her ignorance was the opposite of what we wished. She saw them and just assumed that we all were friends. Yet, the rest of our company were not eager to see the Bingleys at all. Sadly, Elena didn't know that we didn't want to be polite.

"Then we are perfectly met," Miss Bingley said, "let us all dine together."

We all were obliged to accept this. Sometimes having manners cost too much.

Miss Bingley and Mrs. Hurst showered false flattery on Miss Darcy, who tolerated their superficiality with equanimity. I saw behind all their facades. Kitty was not spoken to at all, and soon Elena discovered that perhaps she didn't like the Bingley sisters either. She gathered the impression that, all except Mr. Bingley, did not like Kitty and me. Elena had respect for me, but she was clearly very devoted to Kitty. Therefore, to see most of the Bingley company ignore Kitty altogether did not make a good first impression.

And then there was the subject of Jane. First, I felt apprehensive for her, because now Mr. Bingley was in Brighton, and that was another thing that she did not need.

"This has got to be the worst getaway of all time," I whispered to her. "You were supposed to be free of all this."

"I suppose I have to make do in the best way that I can," Jane whispered in reply. "I will survive this."

Every now and again, Miss Bingley bestowed a sweet word toward Jane. Jane replied peacefully and inquired about what her life had been like since they had left Hertfordshire, but an obvious break was between them. Jane was aware of the Bingley sisters' true nature, and there was no way to go back to the way they were.

The dinner passed without an awkward pause between us, because we were all so desperate to not have uncomfortable silences.

When the dinner came to an end, we all went back to our hotel, with promises to meet the next day and have an excursion.

We parted ways, but Darcy invited Elena, Kitty, Jane, Georgiana and I to sit in his room, where we could play cards. This request was done in secret, unheard by the Bingley party, and we all agreed.

In his room's dining area, we sat down to cards in the candlelight, and the servants brought us a shrub.

"So," Elena began as we played, "that was a family that you all were acquainted with while in Hertfordshire."

"Yes," Kitty said, "for better or for worse."

"Kitty," I reprimanded.

"Sorry, but you were all thinking it. Georgiana, I am sorry, because I know the Bingley sisters are your most particular friends, but I confess that I have had a very different experience with them."

"I can understand," Georgiana said. "They are very kind to me, but if your experience was different, then I cannot begrudge you."

"Kitty," I pressed. "While I do not wish to censor your speeches on the Bingleys, I just do not want Miss Elena's perspective to be shaped around ours. We should let her meet the Bingleys tomorrow and form her own opinion of them."

"Thank you," Elena said, "but I have already formed my own opinions of them. If it is not inappropriate to tell you my findings, then I shall proceed. I found Mr. Bingley to be artless and overall agreeable. Mr. Hurst looks like a gentleman, but he seems like the sort who grumbles through life. And the Bingley sisters... Miss Bennet, Mr. Darcy and Georgiana, I can see that they were very kind toward you, but their praises didn't feel like they were organic. They felt artful and fleeting. They just seemed like they are the sort to forget a friend once that friend has served its purpose."

"You've painted their portrait very well," I determined. "With them, tread carefully."

"The Bingley sisters and Mr. Hurst can always have improved their character," Jane offered, "and we must give them the benefit of the doubt. However, it is always wise to be on one's guard, so that no one is surprised by any sort of behavior."

"But what of the Daltons?" Kitty asked. "We are country folk, so we have little acquaintance in town. Mr. Darcy and Georgiana, who are they?"

"They are a husband and wife in the ton, and they are leaders in the fashionable world," Mr. Darcy explained. "From what I recall of them, they do not like the country, and they are pleasant people. Their chief downside is their extravagance. They are quickly running themselves into debt. But of course, that will not stop them from giving parties."

"Do they have any other resources than just their inheritance?" I asked.

"Perhaps they do, and I am ignorant of it."

"What is certain is that we will be invited," Georgiana confirmed. "We always get invited to the Daltons' balls, and the letter most likely will be re-directed."

"But will the Daltons wish us to be there?" Kitty asked. "For they do not like the country, and we are a country family."

"You will be with us," Mr. Darcy assured us, "and with the Bingleys. Very quickly, they will not care where you are from."

"And what of this Sir Aleck?" Elena asked. "Is he a nice man?"

"So kind that he is quite possibly the most famous man in the aristocracy," Georgiana informed her. "Elizabeth, Jane and Kitty, you met him. You can confirm this."

"Confirm indeed," Kitty said, "when we first met, he had no reason to think me special in any way. But he was kind to me, made particular attention to us all, and was very agreeable."

"He is indeed possessed with such happy manners that he makes anyone feel special, while making all feel special," I noted.

"And therein is our chief difference," Mr. Darcy said. "He is a good man, and very charming, but sometimes that charm can be misdirected."

"In what way?" Jane asked.

"As Lizzy said, he makes one feel special, then he makes everyone feel special. That is why I have a theory that he is the best man to be friends with, but the worst man to be in love with: for you don't know if he pays attention to a woman in the common way, or because he feels a particular attachment to her."

"I see your reasoning," I said, "but like you, I cannot help but be happy to have him in our lives. Darcy, will you and Georgiana accept? Are we going to the ball?"

Mr. Darcy squinted.

"Did I give the impression that I was ever going to turn it down?" he asked. "Oh, I should have stated it before. Yes, we must accept."

"Must?" Kitty repeated. "I want to believe that you are like us, and that you miss Sir Aleck."

"Very well, I do, in part. No more and no less."

"Thank goodness that you bought us new gowns," Jane pointed out, "for I do not believe that we will have been prepared for something so extravagant."

At last, we retired, and Jane and I were undressing in our room.

"So," I began.

"Yes?" Jane said, removing her stockings.

"Mr. Bingley is here."

"Yes, he is."

"Jane, you cannot deceive me. I know that Mr. Bingley's presence disconcerted you."

"Yes, and I had no choice but for it to. I am amazed at this all. We came here for a list of reasons. But one of the reasons that I was so happy was because I would have time to get away from them both. Only for them both to be pulled here. For pulled they were. It is as if Fate wants us to be uncomfortable."

I laughed at her joke.

"Yes, she does seem to be playing a cosmic joke on you three. Perhaps fate is bored right now and has nothing else better to do."

"Yes, perhaps fate desires to be here in Brighton. I am aware that I didn't speak much at dinner, but I needed time to adjust."

"Naturally," I pointed out, removing my stays. "Time indeed!"

"When I see them again tomorrow, I shall know my own strength and can meet him as a common acquaintance."

"Jane," I said, sitting down next to her. "You can try, and I welcome it. But there is the possibility that you will never be fully comfortable."

"That's what scares me. What if I never am able to do so?"

Laying down on her bed, she looked up at the ceiling.

"I cannot believe that I am saying this, but I wish that Mr. Bingley had not come. As well as his pernicious sisters."

I laughed.

"You just said an unkind word of someone!"

"Well, they have given me little choice. After all this time, we have seen Caroline and Louisa."

"Yes, we have."

"It feels like a lifetime since we saw them."

"It's because it has been. We lost our father, Mr. Collins died, Charlotte Lucas lives at Rosings Park, we still might lose Longbourn, Mr. Wickham proposed to me, I got engaged to Mr. Darcy, you received two proposals, we are living with Mr. Darcy and Georgiana, Kitty is writing a book, and we now have Miss Elena Darcy—the woman who pulled herself out of an elopement. The reason that it feels like ages have risen and fallen since we last saw the Bingleys, is because it has. We could write a book with all that's happened."

"Kitty *is* doing that."

"Yes, she is."

I put on my nightgown and then I laid down in my bed.

"There is one thing that also amazed me," Jane said.

"And what is that?"

"Well, Miss Bingley was partial to Mr. Darcy, this cannot be denied. I am surprised that she was able to meet us all with such strength of composure and ease. She displayed no anxiety of your good fortune."

"Yes, we have to give that to her credit."

I blew out the candle on the bedside table and we laid down in darkness.

Yet, somewhere, in the pitch black of night, I was able to see everything clearly.

"Jane?"

"Yes?"

"You are correct. She should have met me with more contempt. It would have been thinly veiled, but it still should have manifested itself. She couldn't help herself, after all."

"But she has."

"Or maybe she doesn't know that we are engaged."

"But how? Surely, Mr. Bingley would have told her?"

"Would he? Think about it. Would he really have wanted to be near her when she heard that news?"

Jane was silent at first.

"She probably does not know!"

"No, she probably doesn't. Neither does Mrs. Hurst too, probably."

I expelled a sigh.

"When the Bingleys arrived in Hertfordshire all those months ago, I never would have foreseen how much they would be entangled in our lives."

"Neither would I," I agreed. "I do not say this as if it were a flaw, but merely as a fact. Their entrance into our lives made everything so complicated from the very beginning. If I did not enjoy the journey we have undergone, I would wonder if maybe father would have done better to have never called on Mr. Bingley from the very beginning."

"Even if so, I believe that it may have all turned out the same. Elizabeth, what happened at the deposition?"

Goodness!

"I just realized that we never had the time to tell you all about it," I remarked.

"No. And I have been curious about it."

"Jane, it proved that no matter how complicated our lives get, there are always more complex stories in the end."

"What will happen to Mr. Wilson?"

"He apologized to Elena, but it is hard to tell if he was sincere or not. But his fate is certain. He will be flogged fifteen times."

"That will be most painful."

"It is a lesson that needs to be learned. Mr. Wilson is not the cold villain that we wish that he was. Yes, he is not the stuff of gothic novels. But he will serve as a great example."

"How so?"

"His punishment will scare any other mercenary officers from eloping. I only wish that Mr. Wickham had seen such an example before he attracted Mary King."

"Wickham will always regret you."

"That is the only thing that keeps me from despising him. Oh, and by the way, Mr. Wilson?"

"Yes?"

"That is not his real name."

"What!"

"Yes, and here is the story."

I proceeded to tell her the entire story, and she was surprised after each moment.

# CHAPTER 15

## THE OUTBURST

The next day, we met the Bingleys for breakfast in the hotel's dining hall. While we ate, I noted that Miss Bingley saw and focused on the fact that Mr. Darcy and I were seated next to each other. Between that and how close we were the night before, it must have made her mind race. My assumption was correct; she was unaware.

When we finished eating, we went to get our coats, cloaks, and bonnets. Assuring the Bingleys that we would meet them in front of their rooms, we gathered our things and were prompt.

Our meeting them there was the best thing, for the next ten minutes would prove to be the worst ten minutes that could ever occur to us in public. Or even in private, for that matter.

As Caroline Bingley and Mrs. Hurst were exiting their rooms, we all were standing there.

"I was just telling Louisa that we must endeavor to make you all proud of us, and have lovely gowns for the ball," Miss Bingley began. "On our outing, Miss Elena, you must point out any shops that you may know about here in Brighton. Your knowledge of the place will prove to be vital to me."

"I shall be delighted," Elena said, "and I can tell you the very best place. It is the same place that we have purchased our bridesmaid dresses and where Elizabeth is getting her wedding gown."

Ah, the information of Elena Darcy! She had been the means through which the Bingleys had eaten dinner with us, and now was the means through which they learned the truth. And I didn't even have to deliver the news myself.

"Married?" Miss Bingley said, stopping in her tracks. "Miss Elizabeth?"

"Yes," I said, "I am to be married. To Mr. Darcy."

Mr. Bingley looked down at the floor.

Mrs. Hurst looked overwhelmed.

Miss Bingley looked as if she had been slapped across the face.

Mr. Hurst looked like he smelled something that was rotten in the state of Denmark. Then again, he looked like that often.

"What!" Miss Bingley gasped, looking between Mr. Darcy and me. "How can this be?"

"He proposed and I accepted," I answered. "Often it is in the usual way."

"Usual way?" she echoed. "Don't make me laugh. This has to be a joke!"

"It is no joke," Mr. Darcy added. "I can assure you. Miss Bingley, will you wish us well?"

"Well? Well!"

"Caroline—" Mr. Bingley began, but Miss Bingley cut him off.

"How can I wish you well when you destroy yourself so? What are the Bennets? What are they that you sacrifice your pride and family's name for them?"

"How can you speak so?" Kitty replied. "We are our father's daughters. He was a gentleman. Therefore, we are a gentleman's daughters."

"But who is your mother? And that's the main sin, your mother! And who are your aunts and uncles? What are they?"

"We are no less in the world than you."

"And who are you to forget that your family's wealth was also acquired through trade?" I added.

"Precisely," Mr. Bingley continued, "our father worked hard to make us what we are. Caroline, how dare you disparage them for being lesser than us, when in my estimation, they are better?"

"And you will cease to defame my new family," Mr. Darcy replied, through gritted teeth. "You will apologize."

"Apologize?" she spat. "You are the one who should be apologizing to me. All this time that I have known you, I have flattered you, praised you, weathered your bad temper and your coldness, and willing to accept you at your worst."

"I never asked this of you," Mr. Darcy responded. "I never asked for your obsequiousness."

"You never had to!" Caroline Bingley responded, clearly heartbroken. "That is what a woman does when she cares."

"You never cared for me, Miss Bingley, but of what you could gain by marrying me."

"How little you know. Why do you think that I hated Elizabeth so quickly? Why do you think I despised a woman who gave me no reason to despise her? It was because I saw you slowly replacing me with her!"

This confession was so disarming that even I was silenced. Miss Bingley was on a getaway cart and she clearly couldn't stop herself. All of her inner feelings and resentment were pouring forth, and she was releasing it all. It was like watching a possessed person exorcise the demon that was in them. But for this new development? Initially, I had thought that she despised me because she believed me to be inferior. But her animosity had sprung from jealousy. She didn't like me, because she saw that Mr. Darcy was falling in love with me… and I merely got caught in the crossfire.

"And for you to have never noticed me, or cared," Miss Bingley continued, her eyes filled with emotion, "for you to do that, Mr. Darcy, displays a coldness in you that is worse than any I ever known. You are not so very great. You are all marble and stone, and I despise you now. And to through me over for a woman who you claimed to not care for initially, and who did not care for you, makes no sense to me. I was here the entire time, doing everything that I could to be perfect for you, and you never saw me. You never saw me at all! But you saw a lesser woman than myself, and it will not be borne."

"But it will be," Jane said at last. "My sister has just as much a right to be loved by any man she chooses, as do you. I bore your incivility toward her with generosity until now, because I saw the good in you, but now I see there is none. It is perfectly natural for you to feel jilted and hurt for losing someone that you loved. But what is improper is for you to be cruel to my sister because the man you loved chose her. We women, like men, must be better than that. And you are not. But for you to really have despised my worthy sister this entire time, only reaffirms that I had been deceived in you. The woman that I had viewed as a good friend was a woman of my imagination. It was not you, Miss Bingley. Not you. You are not familiar to me. For you are a false friend. I do not know you now. And perhaps, it is better that I never come to know you."

This response was the final blow for Caroline. Pain and heartbreak filled her eyes and she took one last look at Mr. Darcy.

"Look at me," she cried, "this is what you have turned me into. This is what you turned me into! A woman as evil as you!"

With that, she ran back into her room, slamming the door behind us, and we all looked at each other awkwardly.

"I guess that means that we shall not go on an excursion today," Mr. Hurst said, still sounding bored.

"For god sakes," Mrs. Hurst groaned, turning to her husband. "Does anything ever affect you? Do you ever care about anything?"

Mr. Hurst scoffed, shocked that she spoke thus to him.

"No," Mrs. Hurst said, "you don't. I married a block of dirt."

With that, Mrs. Hurst went after her sister, to give her company.

"What is everyone's problem all of a sudden?" Mr. Hurst asked.

"Go and see to your wife and my sister," Mr. Bingley said, with more gravity and soberness than we ever heard him. "I'll be in there shortly to help." Mr. Hurst stood there, confused. Somehow, this lack of action incited an anger in Mr. Bingley. For the first time in his life, he had been pushed into having a temper. "Go to it, man! You married into this family, and you married my sister under the condition of for better or worse. Now we are for worse. So how about you try?"

Mr. Bingley's authoritative tone was so startling that Mr. Hurst could not bring himself to question it. He went to Caroline's door and then turned to us.

"You all mistake me," Mr. Hurst said. "I know that you must look on me as if I am nothing else but a lump of nothingness. But when I speak, no one ever thinks my words have any worth, so I stopped trying. Even my own wife can't stand to hear my voice. A person can get tired of that. Also, I learned that if I start to care about something, then I will have to learn to care about anything. And I couldn't do that either. The prospect was too frightening. Too frightening."

He opened the door, and we heard Caroline's lamentations from within, then he closed the door and we were bathed in silence once more. His parting words were another shocking revelation on top of all the other ones, and we felt that we couldn't endure anymore.

Mr. Bingley turned to us, red in the face.

"I am mortified."

"Their actions are not yours," I assured him. "We cannot always control our family."

"Miss Elizabeth," he said, "my sisters may never say it, so I shall. I am heartily ashamed at their treatment of you, and your family. I have always enjoyed your family's kindness, openness, and warmth. If you will allow it, then I will always view you as friends."

"We shall do the same," Jane coaxed, "and tell Miss Bingley that we are not the sort to forsake anyone forever. When she is willing to apologize to my sister, and right the wrongs that she has been long committing, then our bonds can begin to heal."

Mr. Bingley stared longingly at her. Blushing under the weight of his gaze, Jane looked at the floor.

Finally, Mr. Bingley turned to Darcy.

"Darcy, I…"

"It is well," Mr. Darcy said, needing no explanation. "Go to your sister. We'll see you tomorrow."

"Thank you."

Mr. Bingley bowed to us and then he went to Caroline.

Now alone in the hall, we all let out a sigh of exhaustion.

"Well," Elena said, breaking the silence. "I am not entirely sure what just happened. Is there any chance that one of you will explain it to me?"

"I'd say that it is a long story," Kitty said, "but we do have time."

"This is 1807 and we are gentlemen or gentleman's daughters," I finalized. "We have all the time in the world."

"I suppose that our excursion has lost its luster," Georgiana magnified, "but we must not be downhearted. How about we walk along the sand and shore? The water crashing down in waves can often be just as captivating as any monument. For what are man's works when compared to the powers of nature?"

"That is as good an idea as any," I complimented her. "Everyone, would you all be willing?"

"Water is cathartic," Kitty considered, "and we may not be able to bathe in it but seeing it may help do the trick."

We left the hotel and walked to the shore, stepping out onto the sand and remaining close to the water, but not so close that we got splashed.

During the way, Kitty, Jane and I told Elena about our past with the Bingley family. After learning this, she remarked at our ability to even meet them with such civility.

"While Mr. Bingley is a nice man, Jane," Elena said, "I do not deny, that if a man fell in love with me, displayed every symptom of being willing to propose, but did not, then I would not be so kind to him."

"It was difficult for him," Jane explained.

"And I was partly to blame," Mr. Darcy said, "worried that Miss Bennet did not feel for him, I was worried that the feeling between them was not mutual."

"Well," Jane said, "I did hide my feelings a little too much sometimes. I didn't see it at the time."

"Ah," Elena said, "now I know the whole story. I confess that Miss Bingley's outburst does make me feel a little better about myself."

"Why?" Georgiana asked.

"Miss Bingley's exclamations were ill-judged, ill-conceived, and improper to say the least. She was a woman who was crazed from disappointed affections. That is her letting her sensibilities go too far. I have done the same, Georgiana. Sometimes, when you have fallen in some way, it's nice to see others fall, because misery loves company. It's a terrible thing to admit, I know."

"But it is true, nonetheless," Kitty said. "When at home, I clung to Lydia, because I was miserable under the weight of not being anyone's favorite sister."

"Kitty!" Jane gasped. "We never thought less of you."

"Father loved Lizzy the most," Kitty said, "and while mama loved Lydia, it was your beauty that she praised as the jewel as the county, as well as often being known for saying that you were worth more than all of us. My mediocrity and inefficiency were constantly pointed out to me. Lydia was never very accomplished at anything, so we banded together, because, as Elena said, misery loves company."

"We did not know this," I remarked. "You never told us."

"There was no room for it. Well, the beneficial side to it all is that it has given me many words to my feelings, and many feelings to put on the page. Perpetual happiness does not make good writing. To tell a story... you have to have experienced your share of disappointment, failure, inadequacy, inequality or loss. I have felt all those things. So, I have a story."

"Well," I said, "at least our family's shortcomings gave you something."

"It did. Ironically, I am grateful for that."

Up ahead, Kitty found a lovely shell, and she picked it up. This left all our sisters to move ahead of us and look for more shells that might have washed up along the seashore. When doing so, they stuffed them into their reticules, and continued their search.

With my arm in Darcy's, I watched them, amused. Then I looked up at him, expecting him to feel better, but his brow was furrowed.

"Darcy?" I asked. "Are you still thinking about what happened?"

"It feels impossible not to think about it."

"True. But you have said little the whole time that we have

been walking along. What are your thoughts? You know that it is better to speak than keep it silent."

"It is just… remember when Miss Bingley said that I made her like me?"

I was determined and quick to contradict this.

"She was speaking from a place of heartache and passion. She did not know what she was saying."

"I think she did. And Elizabeth…I think that she was right."

"What are you talking about? How could she be right?"

"There is the chance that Miss Bingley was very snobbish and judgmental before she met me. But, even if so, perhaps I encouraged it. When meeting her, I was a mixture of many vices; pride and prejudice being amongst them. I was easily proud of my lineage, my position in society and my connections. I looked meanly on those who I deemed lesser than myself. I even did that with you. All while I did this, Miss Bingley watched. She added support to my thoughts and words. She was like the perfect parrot, and I never discouraged it. After all, why would I? She was echoing sentiments that I voiced, and perhaps that I placed in her? I'm even the cause for why she was so harsh to you. Maybe she chose to become the way she did, because I set a poor example. The metamorphosis of her character might be my fault."

I looked ahead and considered this. There was logic in this, I could not deny. Out of my desire to support Mr. Darcy, I did not want to quickly agree with him. If I did, he would not see the depths of his ability to persuade others, for better or for worse. Yet, I didn't have to agree or disagree. There was a middle path that could be taken, and I wished to offer this as a solution.

"Very well," I said, "since I was not acquainted with you when you met Miss Bingley, I cannot deny that there is the possibility that she learned from any example that you gave. But here is something that you need to consider: every man and every woman's soul is their own. You may have influenced her, but she was the one who chose to be influenced. She is a grown woman. She can make up her own mind about things. Her choosing to be influenced by you is still *her* choice. The right to *choose* is the most powerful right in the world. By taking it away from herself and making it solely dependent on your good opinion, was *her* not being fair to herself. We have fallen in love, correct? Yes, we have. And in all that while, did I blindly agree with you on anything? Never. I wish to be in accordance with you, but if I disagree with you about something, then I will not change my opinion just to suit yours. We are all responsible for our own actions. You didn't tell her that she had to hate me. She chose to do it herself. So whatever lessons you may have taught her, she was at the age where she could have said 'never mind, I will teach myself'. At some point, we all have to grow up and say that. This will be her chance to define herself, instead of defining herself by how she fits around you."

He looked down at me, his face relaxing.

"A weight has been lifted off my shoulders."

"There," I said. squeezing his arm, "you are yourself again. And so am I."

"Brother and Lizzy, look!" Georgiana called. We turned to her as she was raising up a seashell. "Spoils of the sea!"

It was the most beautiful shell that I had ever seen.

"Well done!" I cried. "Keep it forever!"

Walking along more, I turned and glimpsed the water. The tide rolled in and out. Amongst the water, I saw glimpses of seaweed, twigs, shells and other elements of the sea. Looking ahead, the water met the horizon, with the sun getting closer and closer to the drink, its reflection stretched across the surface.

Further away, there were ships traversing it, meeting trade or conflict.

It was amusing to think that their struggles perhaps, were no greater and smaller than those we had on shore. But with the coming and going of the waves crashing against the sand, we did find peace and a moment away from all the noise that met us everywhere else.

Returning to the hotel, we ate dinner in Mr. Darcy's room again, then we removed our shoes and placed them in front of the fire so that they could get warmer.

Seeing our feet all lined up like that was amusing. Resting my head on Mr. Darcy's shoulders, I stared into the fire.

"Fire and water," I whispered, "one warms and the other cleanses."

"Feel born anew yet?" Mr. Darcy asked me.

"Better than new," I remarked.

The fire crackled and continued until it was time to retire.

# CHAPTER 16

## TIME TO SMILE AGAIN

The next day, Colonel Fitzwilliam called on us, and wondered if we would be willing to go to Ditchling Beacon, which was a nice area of land that stretched far, and you could see the sea and land for miles around. It was on raised land, where there were pathways and wonderful views.

"Finally!" Elena cried. "Each time that I wished to take them, something else got in the way. Colonel, you have helped me return to my intention."

"We would be delighted," I said, also to Mr. Darcy. "Can we go?"

"Of course," Mr. Darcy said, "but Richard, there is something of importance that I have to tell you."

"Another important thing?" Colonel Fitzwilliam said. "Brighton continues to offer new things."

"This time it is not new things, but older acquaintances. Have you heard of the Dalton's ball?"

"Oh, yes. I have. I was meaning to ask if you all are going?"

"If we receive the invitation, then yes. We shall."

"Oh, you will," he added with a smirk. "The invitation has to find you first."

"Either way, to help with the preparations, the Daltons have invited Sir Aleck Granger and his family. It turns out, that Miss Dalton is particular friends with Miss Bingley. Thus, the Bingleys

157

were invited to come, and Mr. Charles Bingley was obligated to join as well. They arrived a couple of days ago and are staying here in the Grand Brighton."

"Ah," Colonel Fitzwilliam responded. His tone was ambiguous. An outside observer would have thought that he was amenable to this idea. A person who was more acquainted with his character would know better, which is that he did not know how to receive this new development. "Well, shall we extend the invitation?"

"Not this day," Mr. Darcy said. "For they might already be engaged with the Daltons. It will suffice just to leave a note for them. I need a couple minutes to write it myself."

"Splendid."

Mr. Darcy wrote a brief note, ordered it to be sent to Mr. Bingley's room, then we departed in a carriage.

---

"Is there anything superior in the world to this?!" Kitty cried as we stood on the highest part of Ditchling Beacon.

"It does seem as if we are seeing the entire world from here," Jane said next to her, "and how peaceful it is."

I felt the wind on my face. "When I look out, I am seeing my entire life stretch out before me."

And we all really did. From our view, we saw sweeping lands, quaint homes in the distance, and the blueness of the sky as the sun cast its rays on the lands. It felt as if we all could leave everything behind. For we all had a right to.

Initially, we all stood there, just gazing at the beauty that was before us, and then we walked along, past a few trees.

"What are the works of man when compared to the beauties of nature?" Georgiana asked, referring to what we mentioned earlier.

"It is what my grandmother once said to me when I was a boy," Colonel Fitzwilliam said. "Give me a comfortable home, a purpose in life, and a rocking chair to sit in when I behold the splendor of nature, and everything else will work itself out."

"Your grandmother liked rocking chairs?" Jane asked. "I do as well."

"I never met a sensible woman who didn't," Colonel responded, smiling.

"When you say your grandmother," Elena asked, "is she also your grandmother, Mr. Darcy?"

"I don't recall our grandmother saying that," Mr. Darcy determined.

"It was my grandmother on my mother's side," Colonel explained. "Darcy and I are related through my father. I am heartily sorry that she wasn't your grandmother, Darcy. She was a lovely and large jolly woman. The perfect sort of woman for a grandson who was crying because he scraped his knee. The larger they are, sometimes the more giving. She would scoop me up in her embrace and I felt as if nothing could ever harm me."

"You had a beautiful childhood," Kitty observed. "Our grandparents were delightful too, weren't they Jane and Lizzy?"

"Oh, grandmas," I sighed. "We never knew our father's parents, because they died before we were born. But our mother's parents were irreplaceable. It was our grandmother who taught us how to read."

"Really?" Mr. Darcy asked.

"Yes. Even in her old age, she wanted to make sure that we could read and write as good as anyone."

"And then she began to go blind," Jane recalled. "It felt like our world went black with her."

"Yes, it did," I recalled. "And grandfather worked so hard almost every day, right up until the day he died. But he never missed any of our birthdays."

"Neither of them did," Kitty said. "It wasn't fair that they didn't get to see us grow up. Elena, Georgiana, Mr. Darcy and Colonel, our grandmother passed away when I was ten, and our grandfather followed her a month later."

"Did he die of a broken heart?" Elena asked.

"We believe so."

"I overheard our Aunt Phillips tell a different tale," Jane revealed. "One time, I heard her and mother talking. It turns out that our grandfather was sick for a long time. They said that he fought to live until she left first, to make sure that her last days in life were not her having to be told that her home was no longer hers. Of course, it went to our Uncle Gardiner, and he deserved it more than anyone. But grandfather wanted to shield grandmother till the day he died."

"Your grandfather died a great man," Colonel Fitzwilliam determined.

"He was like you and Mr. Darcy," I said. "You would have loved him. And I just realized that we have made the scene turn dour, haven't we?"

"Not at all," Mr. Darcy assured me. "Beautiful scenes can bring forth beautiful memories."

Colonel Fitzwilliam analyzed us all, from Jane on one arm, Georgiana on the other, then me on Mr. Darcy's arm, and Elena on the other, leaving Kitty to be the only one to walk alongside us.

"That is the problem with having only two gentlemen with five ladies," he observed. "Not enough arms to link with."

We all laughed, and Kitty took no offense.

"Hello there!" We heard from further off. Looking to where we were called, we were surprised to see that it was Sir Aleck Granger.

"Well, this is a pleasant surprise," Sir Aleck called to us as he walked along.

"And just when we thought we women greatly outnumbered the men in our company," Kitty laughed. "Sir Aleck, how did you find us?"

"On the contrary, Miss Kitty," Sir Aleck responded, removing his hat, "you are the lovely sprites who found me."

"Sir Aleck," Mr. Darcy said, "allow me to introduce you to my cousin, Miss Elena Darcy."

Sir Aleck turned to Elena, and he blinked. It was made very evident that he was struck by her smile and beauty.

"Miss Elena, the pleasure is all mine," Sir Aleck said as she curtsied.

"Don't I know it?" she asked. This response made him laugh. "I hope that I have made you comfortable."

"You have. Mr. Darcy, all this time and you had a charming cousin."

"That I met for the first time a couple weeks ago," Mr. Darcy augmented. "Therefore, I kept nothing from you at all."

"I was the one who was kept from them," Elena elaborated, "but it has all worked out in the end. For now, as you see, we are all walking along Ditchling as if we have always known each other."

"Sir Aleck," Mr. Darcy acknowledged, "I've heard tales of you coming to Brighton."

"And those tales are all true, as you see. And by you being here, I can see that you might not have gotten the Daltons invitation."

"In the case that it does not get forwarded to the Grand Brighton, can you tell the Daltons that I will attend with a party of six, including Richard?"

"I can do that very well."

"And what brings you to Ditchling?" I asked. "Have you come to meet someone?"

"No, this time I walk alone," Sir Aleck said. "Even the social need time to get away from society. I daresay that you know it often is so. We all crave for people around us, but sometimes nothing can compare to the beauties of solitude."

"The question is how to find the perfect balance for it," Elena continued, "for I had long been left to solitude when I was a child. Therefore, want of society was my condition, and if you are the popular man that you appear to be, then looking for loneliness is yours."

"So, where do we gain?" he asked. "Where is the balance to this problem?"

"I cannot tell you, but I wish that I could."

"An honest answer. I would have preferred it that way."

"Would you like to join our company?" Kitty asked, her voice a little eager. "Or do you wish to find the solitude that you sought after?"

"A difficult question," Sir Aleck said, still looking at Elena. "I do not know what to do, for yes, I wish for peace and quiet, but when presented with such delightful company, how can I resist?"

"A difficult path," Kitty continued. "Which one suits you more?"

"Whatever choice you make, we will not judge you," I assured him.

Sir Aleck put his hat on and offered Elena his right arm. She placed hers in his.

"I have made my choice," he said. Then he turned to Kitty and offered his other arm to her, as an afterthought.

Aware of this, Kitty placed her arm in his and accepted it with lesser enthusiasm.

---

With the new addition to our party, I had the time to observe everyone.

Sir Aleck was being his traditionally charming self. This time, his focus was primarily on Elena. Every now and again, he focused on Kitty, but it was made very evident that Sir Aleck was now absorbed in his new acquaintance.

"Do you see what I see?" I asked Darcy.

"Yes," Mr. Darcy said, "I do. Kitty should not take it personally. Sir Aleck is always very kind and attentive when he meets new people. He is always eager to make a new friend."

"But at the expense of making his older friends feel neglect?"

"Sir Aleck is a wonderful man, but like I said, that is the trouble with charming people. They treat everyone special…"

"So no one is. Yes, now I see what you meant. Either way, that will be a poor excuse for Kitty. It doesn't matter what he is. I get the suspicion that she did favor him when they met. Perhaps it was larger than she let on. Maybe she was looking forward to seeing him again. And now she is discovering that he was more significant to her, than she was to him. It's not a lovely feeling. And you know his character better than we do. Darcy, do you think I should talk to Kitty about this?"

"Yes. The last thing that she needs is to be left in the dark, and possibly become a pale reflection of Miss Bingley."

This point did alarm me.

After all, feeling passed over leads to insecurity, and seeing the woman who replaced you leads to resentment. I didn't want that to happen to Kitty.

"I'll talk to her."

Directing my attention to Colonel Fitzwilliam, he was speaking very comfortably with Jane and Georgiana. You would never think, by looking at him, that he had accepted Jane's lack of commitment of his hand, by the way that they were talking. If the Colonel could recover and believe that there was life after love, then so could Kitty.

"All things can often turn out well, in the end."

# CHAPTER 17

## DOES THIS CONVERSATION CAUSE YOU PAIN?

*S*ir Aleck returned to the hotel and was very pleasant company, but his charm was still mostly directed to Elena, who received his attentions eagerly.

Kitty was a little quieter at dinner, sitting next to Georgiana. But once Georgiana engaged her in conversation, Kitty threw herself into their talk with alacrity. I deduced that her eagerness was the result of being happy that something was there to distract her from the fact that Sir Aleck's attention did not belong to her at all. Yet, I was still unsure of if I was deducing things correctly.

Once the dinner ended, I asked Jane if she could invite Georgiana to our room, so that I could speak to Kitty in secret. Jane accepted this, for she too saw a marked difference in Kitty's behavior.

When alone with Kitty, I began to tend to the fire, to make it larger, while she began to undo her hair.

"You came to see me in confidence," she noticed. "Now, why would Lizzy do that? Are you about to ask me if I put any of the recent events into my book?"

"No. I come with a more pressing matter," I said, cutting to the point. "I came to ask you about how you are feeling. I saw how Sir Aleck's attentions toward Elena affected you."

Kitty lowered her hands as her hair fell around her face.

"You saw that?" she asked.

"Yes, I did."

Kitty closed her eyes.

"I thought that I hid it from everyone. But you all saw it?"

"Don't worry. You didn't make a spectacle of yourself. I am not here to lecture you or chastise you for having emotions. I am here to tell you that if you need someone to talk to, then I am here. And then, if I can, I will try to help."

"You will not call me foolish or silly?"

"Never. This is something that is clearly important to you."

Kitty removed her shoes and then sat still.

"I thought that he found me special," Kitty began. "And that he might have enjoyed my company."

"I am sure that he did. Miss Elena is new to him, and therefore a novelty. Some people love novelties, especially if they feel exotic. His current actions now do not dictate how they will always be."

"So, I should hope that he will change?"

"Oh, no!" I denied. "Do not ever hope a man or woman to change over time just because you want them to. Usually, they have either come to you with their character developed, or they have to change because they are doing it for themselves. Sir Aleck is a man who is as he will always be. His character is set, defined and developed into this. He is a kind, generous, unassuming, and warm-hearted person. But his lovely traits are there for everyone. And as a result, he will lure you in, innocently, and then you will spend your time watching him bestow his attentions on everyone else, while you are waiting for him to direct them back to you. That is no way to spend your time. Popular men like that can be miserable to fall in love with. For, since they treat everyone special, they treat no one special."

"It is worse than that."

"How?"

"When I saw him with Elena, I was…"

"Jealous?"

"Yes."

Kitty removed her stockings and threw them on the bed.

"I hate myself for feeling it." She tried to unclasp her gown without success, so I helped her.

"I am happy that you told me," I said, "for it is wiser for you to confess this than keep it hidden within you. While you were feeling jealous, did you feel any resentment to Elena?"

"That was the painful thing. She and I have become great friends, and there I was, secretly wishing her to be on the other side of the world. I could not bear to even look at her."

"Kitty, I am going to give that advice now. I know that it will be hard to take this advice, but you need to try. I know that nothing I say will stop you from favoring Sir Aleck. So, I won't say anything. You have every right to like him, even if he prefers other company sometimes. Be happy when you see him. But do not make yourself unhappy if he ever shows attention elsewhere. Find your own joy in other places, most particularly your writing. Do not make yourself unhappy over him. And yes, Elena and you have become good friends. Is a man worth losing that? She needs you now, more than ever. If it turns out that Sir Aleck really does admire her, then do not let that sour your temper. They are not worth you losing your soul to ill-humor. Your main attribute, Kitty, is your open nature. Jealousy and resentment kill natures such as yours."

"I tried to tell myself that, all throughout dinner," Kitty urged. "I tried to tell myself that Elena does like me, and Sir Aleck still is kind to me. But I still could not deny the warning in my heart. Then I thought such evil things of her, and I could not stop myself. I felt as if I was…"

"On the same path that Miss Bingley was on when she saw me."

Kitty lowered her head.

"Yes," she answered, "I felt as if I was falling into that pattern. I saw myself giving way and heading into self-defeat, but I could not stop myself. I stood on the brink and felt as if I was blinded by an eclipse."

"I have been that way before."

"How did you recover from it?"

"I told myself that people were not worth me losing myself over. Your affection for Sir Aleck shows your good taste, but he will *never* be worth you losing your whole spirit to. Just as it is not worth you losing Elena. When you see them together, think of the characters that you are writing about, and focus on them. Dance with other men, find pleasure in other people's company. And then you will recover. And one day, it will no longer hurt. Be Elena's friend. She doesn't know the pain she's causing you."

"You are right. She doesn't. All that she will know is that I am her friend one day, and then I am her enemy the next. No, I will not be like that."

I reached over and hugged her.

"I will not turn into something horrible, just because I might be slighted. I have my characters in my book. Even if things do not work out for me, I can change that. In my writing, my characters will be like me. They will have some trouble, then they will have more trouble. But in the end, unlike me, they will have their happily ever after."

"I believe you will," I said, taking her hand. "But Kitty, I recalled something. When you first told us that you were writing, Mr. Darcy did not look happy."

"He might have been upset at the idea that I am a woman writer. I believe that he will get over that."

"I do not think he ever had a problem with that. I think he was merely thinking of your prospects. Not many men would be interested in marrying a woman writer. I think he was worried that your life would be a little harder because of the choice you made."

"Or perhaps not," she pointed out, hopeful. "Perhaps I might be able to live by my pen. Stranger things have happened. Lizzy, I have to dream now. My dream is the only thing I have left, and the only thing within my control."

"I have faith in you, but do not be upset if your dream fades."

"I won't be. I'm just happy that I have it."

I kissed Kitty on the forehead.

"Have it all you wish."

I left her alone to retire for the evening.

The next day, I was dressed earlier than Jane was. Needing to get her hair done up by Kitty, who was better at applying braids, I was left alone. Now at liberty, I felt emboldened. Spending a life being reactive as opposed to proactive was not meant for me. If life was going to be complicated and lack resolution, it would not be at my hands.

Leaving the room, with a note on Jane's bed, to explain where I was going, I went downstairs to the next floor where I knew the Bingleys were staying. Knocking on Mr. Bingley's door, I only waited for a few seconds before Mr. Bingley opened it.

"Miss Bennet?" he asked, "you have come to see me?"

"I need your help, Mr. Bingley."

"Of course," he insisted, naturally happy to welcome the sister to his beloved. "I shall be happy to help in any way that you need assistance."

"It has to do with your sister, Miss Bingley."

"Yes," he replied awkwardly, "that."

"I am aware of our past."

"Your past is not your fault."

"Thank you, but in the present, I have to try and change the future. You are my fiancé's closest friend. And your sister favors him. If she is left to her own passions, they may build even further. I have seen resentment lead to madness. Now, there is the chance that Miss Bingley will not want to make peace with me, but I must try. If she still keeps to her room, then may you appeal to her on my behalf and see if she will talk to me?"

"I admit that I do not have as much influence on her as Louisa does," Mr. Bingley said. "Remain here, I will go to Louisa's room, and we shall appeal to her together. Do not worry about me being long. You know my nature. I often move too quickly for my own good."

He went down the hall, knocked on Louisa's door, and Mr. Hurst opened it. Louisa quickly came to the door and both had words with each other. Immediately, I saw that Louisa was accepting of the idea, she assured me that they would do everything to convince Caroline to talk to me.

"Miss Bennet," Louisa said, with more congeniality in her tone than she ever had with me before, "it is so generous of you that you wish to resolve things. It is the sort of goodness that I always know to expect from your family."

How the tide had turned!

For one time, she must have been ridiculing my dirty petticoat after I walked to Netherfield. And now she was praising my family.

Truly, sometimes one's fortune varied so much without consequence!

As Mrs. Hurst and Mr. Bingley went into Caroline's room, Mr. Hurst stood in front of his doorway, awkwardly.

"Good day, Mr. Hurst," I said.

"Good day, Miss Bennet," he said, bowing to me, feeling uncertain. "Are you enjoying your stay here in Brighton?"

"Very much. I have enjoyed it immensely. I only wish that I could have come during the summer, when there is a chance at sea-bathing."

"Of course. Sea-bathing is delightful."

"I have been told that it is a wonderful thing."

"You've been told?" he asked, his eyebrow raised. "Then... you have never sea-bathed."

"Not one day in my life."

"Oh, I am heartily sorry for it. Sea-bathing is one of life's best delights. When I was a boy, it was something I looked forward to every year."

"You sea-bathed when you were a child?"

He laughed heartily. That may have been the first time that I ever saw him guffaw. "I loved swimming when I was a boy. And when I couldn't get to the sea, I rushed to any water that there was. My brothers and my sister used to rush to a lake that was near our parents' estate, and we would jump in."

"Really?" I asked, amazed. "You must have been really happy."

"Those were the days," he said, getting a faraway look in his eye. "And then we got older, and it was improper to do those sorts of things anymore."

His brow became furrowed, and I felt as if I saw a cloud return over his head. It was a rain cloud that he probably let reign often on him.

"We grow up too fast," I noted.

"We blink… and then we are told that now we have to spend the rest of our lives, miserable."

We were interrupted when Mr. Bingley and Mrs. Hurst came out of Caroline's room.

"Success," Mrs. Hurst said, "Caroline will see you."

I took some deep breaths to embolden myself.

"I feel as this will all fly back in my face," I admitted.

"If it does, we shall recall that you offered the olive branch," Mrs. Hurst said, "and that will mean all the difference."

"Yes," Mr. Bingley said, "to us, you are as good a friend already."

"Thank you."

Walking up to the door, I prepared myself, and then I opened it.

Taking a few steps, I saw that Miss Bingley was sitting by the window.

When seeing me, she stood up.

"Miss Bennet," she said heavily, her face flushed and her expression grave. Her eyes were a little red and I knew what that signified.

"Miss Bingley."

We curtsied to each other and I closed the door behind me.

"Please," she said, "do be seated."

I sat down at the chair that was opposite hers and folded my hands on my lap.

"How are you?" I asked.

"I am well."

"Miss Bingley," I said, not willing to waste any time, for I knew I would be missed. "Forgive me, but I know that is not true. I can see by your face that you have been crying."

Caroline rubbed her cheek, and she bit her lip.

"You know enough about my frank nature to not be offended, I hope."

"That is perhaps what he likes about you, isn't it? You and he are kindred spirits."

"Perhaps we are. Miss Bingley, I understand why you were

resentful of me. I wish that you were not, but perhaps you had no choice in the matter. We women are like men, in the sense that when our affections are aroused, the subject of our affection leads to us becoming overprotective. And possessive. We feel as if he is our rightful property. Is that what you felt when you saw Mr. Darcy?"

"It was more than that," she said. "When I met him, it felt like destiny. Our father worked hard to put us on the same level as women like Miss Darcy, but we are not. And I have done everything in the world to make sure that people do not look at us as being anything else but a gentleman's daughters. Yet, my father was not a gentleman."

"My mother was not what was regarded as a lady. Nor was my grandfather a gentleman."

"And yet, he chose you," she sighed, closing her eyes, about to cry again.

"Miss Bingley, please," I urged, "do not do that."

"When Mr. Darcy and my brother became friends, it was like fate had brought me the man who was handsome, everything worthy and would fulfill the dream that my father had of his children becoming as great as anyone. He worked so hard for it, and I want to gratify him for it."

"And the only way that you can do that is by marrying well."

"It is all I know. But when I saw Mr. Darcy, I thought it was a duty that would be easy. It was like I was walking into a dream. He and I didn't have much in common, but when has that ever stopped two people from falling in love? So, I thought that my life was finally beginning."

When she opened her eyes again, she was looking ahead, as if she was seeing something far away from us.

"And then we came to Hertfordshire, and everything changed. All it took was one ball, and he met you. At first, he dismissed you, and I felt so secure. Then at Sir William's party, something changed. It was like you placed a spell on him. And that was when it began."

"When you began to hate me?"

"I couldn't control myself. I wished that he had never met you.

And then it continued that way. You walked to Netherfield, and all you came for was for your sister! But he showed affection for you, attention! Attention that I did everything to see that he gave me! Miss Bennet, you know not all the times that he said something, without affection, and I still was kind to him, anyway. I always tried to understand him, even when it was hard. And I felt so betrayed and neglected when he looked past all my praises and cast his eye on you."

She leaned forward so quickly, so sharply, that it disconcerted me.

"What did you have that I didn't?" she asked savagely. "You are not more beautiful than I am. I am more accomplished—and I do not slander you now, Miss Elizabeth. You dance, play and sing very well. I am merely stating facts. You heard him that night, though. When he was listing his requirements for what it meant to be accomplished. I know that I contributed to that list, but he agreed to it. He agreed! I just wasn't a great reader, like you, but what of that? Yes, you are charming, but… aren't I too? So, why am I nothing?" She wept. "Miss Bennet, why am I nothing?"

"Miss Bingley," I explained, taking my time and speaking slowly. Truly, it was like moving slowly when beholding a spooked animal. "You are not nothing. First, that is the problem here. While it is bewitching for one's happiness to be wrapped up in another person, it is not sound. I know that it is our duty in life to marry as well as we can. But there must be more to us than that. We must be whole unto ourselves, even if we are not married. Finding one's partner is *another* aspect of life, but it's not *all* of our life. The more we are acceptable unto ourselves, the more that we are ready for when we do marry. You are correct, you are no less beautiful than I, and more accomplished. Accomplishments, like elegance, are what enhances a man's affection for us, but it doesn't create it. And to be frank, that is a good thing. If a man chooses to love someone because of her accomplishments, he loves her for her talent, and not for her character."

She looked at me, confused.

"And secondly, there are no rules on what attracts two people together. Often, it changes with each set of lovers. I know that no matter what I tell you, your heart will make its own choices. But believe me, you lose no value because of a man falling in love with another. I know that you will feel wrong. But no one is wrong because someone loves someone else instead of them. So, you are not defective in any way if a man places his affections elsewhere. I have been in the situation often where a man preferred Jane over me, and I was never jealous of her for it. I understood that it was natural, and I did not lack anything because of it."

"How did you recover from that?" she asked. "How did you bear seeing Jane be so much admired over you?"

"Easily," I said. "I knew my own merit. We are all modest sometimes, because we should be. We are all flawed, and we should confront it. But I still am fortified. My self-respect is still intact. Also, Miss Bingley, your feelings have led to you being prejudiced against me. What good has that done you?"

She looked away from me.

"No, really, what good has that done? Now you are unhappy, and you made us incapable of being friends. No one is worth you questioning your self-value and hardening your heart against someone else for so insipid a reason. It makes you the uglier for it, when you have it in you to always be a lovely woman."

"Me? Lovely?"

"Yes," I assured her. "You are. You are lovely, accomplished, have your wealth, and you have all the chances in the world to live and love again. And you will."

"Why couldn't you have been evil?" she asked.

"I beg your pardon?"

"It would have been easier if you were evil. I could have something to hate. This is awful to say, but since we are being honest, hating you made it all easier. Now you are showing yourself to be a superior woman. And that makes it harder. I have no choice but to admit that you are perfect for him. And I do not know if I can ever forgive you for that."

"You must understand that I do not ask for forgiveness on that score."

"As you shouldn't. Miss Bennet, I know that you are a worthy woman, but I need time to accept this. Your appearance will antagonize me, and it will only remind me of the woman that I am not, and the woman that he chose. What you have said shows that you are a delight, and I will try to improve. But time needs to assist me. Forgive me, but I need time away from you all, so that when I see you again, I can offer you the respect that you deserve, rather than giving my contempt. I do not want you to see me like this. We both deserve better. And when I do enter your life again, I hope that you will still offer me the olive branch that you have been so kind to bestow now. I will earn your good opinion one day, but not today."

"Very well, I am content with that," I said.

I offered her my farewell and left her alone, comforted at the idea that I did the best I could.

# CHAPTER 18

## A DAY FOR A DANCE

The delightful thing about cities is that even when it rains, there are still places to go and see. But this time, we were larger in number. Never were we in Miss Bingley's company, for she made certain that she spent all her time with Miss Dalton.

Yet, Mr. Bingley, the Hursts and Colonel Fitzwilliam were frequent in their visits with us. Mr. Bingley and Colonel Fitzwilliam found a way to tolerate each other, by the unspoken rule of not showing particular attention to Jane. Colonel Fitzwilliam often spoke with Kitty, and Mr. Bingley talked with Georgiana. Every now and again, they displayed their charm to Jane, but never in a way that disconcerted her.

The only complication was Sir Aleck Granger. When not helping the Daltons plan their ball that would take place at the Royal Pavilion, Sir Aleck immersed himself into our company with the greatest of ease. The man was born to make everyone comfortable when he was there, and longing for his presence when he was absent.

He was among our party when we visited the Preston Manor—and of course, he knew all the people who lived there.

"While I am not that fascinated with beautiful homes," I said as we moved through it, "I cannot deny that this is a lovely place. Mr. Darcy, tell me about Pemberley."

"Miss Elizabeth," he said, "I am happy that I have refrained from showing you my home until after we are married. This way, I can give you the most beautiful surprise."

"I will enjoy it," I said, "no matter what."

We visited the North and South Lanes, which had the most exquisite shops and dining places. We also visited Kempton, St. Bartholomew's church, and the Chattri, which was a lovely monument.

All the while, Sir Aleck attended us, and it would have been perfect, had there been no one tangled in love. For, Sir Aleck always sought out Elena on these excursions, and Elena enjoyed the attention.

I knew that Kitty was in pain over this, but she covered it up most admirably. Or, she saved all her heartache for her writing. I very well knew that she still favored him, because she told me so, in secret.

Yet, since she was not the only one entangled in romantic complications, she had company. Since the Colonel could not express his love for Jane, talking to Kitty was the next best thing. Because of such, he often spoke with her on these excursions, and they were able to provide each other with a distraction.

Although all these romantic tensions lay underneath the surface of our conversations, we were spared any awkward scenes. Therefore, even if our company had elements of pain in it, it still caused pleasure.

A day before the ball, my wedding gown was finished, along with the bridesmaid gowns. We all went to try them on, and when we were shown to Mr. Darcy, he was amazed.

"Do we look worthy of the Master of Pemberley?" I asked.

"More than worthy," he said, his tone serious and sincere. "You all look beautiful."

"And we all feel beautiful." Kitty laughed, grabbing Georgiana's hands and twirling her around. Don't we, Lizzy, Jane and Elena?"

"Yes, we do," Elena answered. "In all my life, this is the first time that I have been in a wedding. I am a part of the family."

Kitty touched her hand and it warmed me to see. No matter what Sir Aleck did, Kitty was always succeeding at not letting it ruin her relationship with her new friend. Naturally, she leaned more toward Georgiana now, but Elena never felt left out.

"We shall have to get gowns made for Lydia and Mary as well when we get back to Hertfordshire," Jane said, "and…"

She trailed off when she saw Mr. Darcy walking up to me slowly. Eventually, he placed his hand on my waist, leaned down and we kissed.

"I think you might still be in love with me," I teased him when our lips parted.

"Is that not the custom of men and women when they are about to marry?"

"It is what is right, but sadly, it is not often the custom. I've seen many a woman and man who walked into marriage as if it was the end, but you are one who I see knows that it is only the beginning of something else."

"We have a ball tomorrow night and a wedding soon afterwards," Georgiana observed. "If only life was always so properly eventful."

"Only if England decided to have a couple married every week of the year," I pointed out. "But until then, we shall have to make do."

"First thing is first," Kitty said, dancing briefly with Jane, then me, then Elena and Georgiana. "We have to hope that we can dance every dance tomorrow. May we all find our good fortune there… as far as amusements go."

"I believe that you shall," I said.

After we had our gowns taken to the hotel, Jane, Kitty, Darcy and I visited Lydia, who was dining with the officers. Naturally, she was still in good spirits, in good looks, and enjoying herself immensely.

"I have found my life here," Lydia boasted.

"And what does that mean?" Jane asked.

"It means precisely what I say!" she teased, with a wicked look in her eye. "If I am not mistaken, I might be married before all of you. What a good joke that would be! I can scarcely breathe for laughing."

Passing it off as one of her fancies—for she had often talked that way at home, we accepted that she was doing as well as could be expected and left her to Mrs. Forster's company. Other than her usual high-spiritedness, we had heard no rumors of her being vulgar, outlandish, or getting in any sort of trouble, so we felt that there was nothing to worry over.

Also, I did not deny that I always preferred her to be in Mr. Darcy's company as little as possible, so not to vex him. Eager to get back to the Grand Brighton and continue thinking happy thoughts of tomorrow evening, was my chief aim.

---

The day of the ball arrived and all of us made certain to eat a tiny breakfast in the morning and had as little to drink throughout the day. For the less that you have in you, the longer you can last at a ball.

When I was combing my hair, Georgiana came to my room, asking me which gown that I preferred. Kitty had given her advice, but Georgiana wanted a second opinion.

"Kitty is correct," I said. "The green one is the better one."

"Good," Georgiana said. "I was hoping you would say so. I liked it as well, but I worried that Kitty and I were wrong."

"Well, you weren't. Sometimes the first instinct is the right one. By the way, how is Kitty doing? Is she happy?"

"She is perfectly well. Why? Are you worried that her feelings for Sir Aleck are affecting her, especially since he prefers Elena now?"

I blinked.

"Oh, she told you as well?"

"No, but I saw what was happening. I know that she liked Sir Aleck, and I know that Sir Aleck likes Elena, so I knew what would follow. At the present time, there is no need for alarm. She is doing very well, and I believe she is over the worst of it. Sir Aleck is a man who many of us women have felt for, in one time or another. Yet, it is an infatuation that usually fades over time."

"You felt for him before?" I asked.

"It was a brief feeling. It died soon. With any luck, Kitty's will fade as well."

"That is good to hear. I do not want her losing her heart over this, or her sense of security. Love can be so disconcerting. Also, I am happy that she has not let this affect her friendship with Elena."

"They do talk less, but not so much that Elena notices. Oh, this next confession is wicked of me!"

"What confession?" I asked, ceasing to comb my hair.

"I am happy that there is a break in their bond. I was happy to help Elena, and I was happy to see her again. But the thought of her becoming so dear to Kitty did not occur to me."

This new development was not something that I saw coming. In fact, I wondered if I was believing my ears.

"Georgiana, dear, were you upset that maybe you were losing Kitty to Elena?"

"Yes. I know that it's not sensible. In fact, Kitty never gave any indication that she was forgetting me. But when Elena entered our lives, I thought that Kitty would still just be bound to me as a close friend. I wasn't ready to share her with anyone else, in particular. At least, now I get my friend back. I know that she never left, but when your close camaraderie changes from the number two to three, you feel an intrusion."

"Well," I said, taking her hand. "I am happy that things have taken a little turn, to everyone's satisfaction. This is good, Georgiana. Now, get prepared for a night of gaiety."

"Yes."

"And Georgiana?"

"Yes?"

"If you ever do feel that you are losing Kitty to someone else, just tell her. She will not feel awkward over it, but rather, she will only try to rectify the injury. She likes you a lot, and she will never want to lose you."

"I suppose that I am not very good at confrontation. But I am learning."

She kissed me on the cheek and went back to her room.

We spent the day bathing, having our faces done up as well as our hair. When the time for the ball arrived, we had our cloaks on and we emerged from our rooms. Mr. Darcy and the Colonel were waiting for us. They looked handsome, but had still not seen our gowns, for we were so covered up.

"We are meeting the Bingleys and Hursts downstairs in the hall," Mr. Darcy said.

Upon going downstairs, we found Mr. Bingley, Mr. Hurst and his sisters there, also wearing their cloaks. They were happy to meet us, but Miss Bingley remained in the background, unwilling to speak much at all.

We got into the carriages and were on our way. I was packed in with Mr. Darcy, Kitty, Elena, and Jane. Colonel Fitzwilliam sat next to the driver on his seat. Georgiana went in the Bingley's carriage with them, and we were off.

Along the way, Kitty removed some pages from her reticule and began to read them to herself.

"Kitty, what is that?" Elena asked.

"Oh," Kitty sighed, "truth is that all today, I had a burst of inspiration and I decided to rewrite the first pages of my novel again. I did so, and I am worried that maybe I am wrong. What if they are terrible?"

"When we get back to the hotel, I am willing to read your new edits."

"You would?" Kitty asked, brightening up. "Oh, that will be very good. Thank you."

She continued to read to herself, for the sun had not fully set yet, and there still was some light peeking through the carriage windows.

We arrived at the Royal Pavilion, disembarked, and were among the crowd of elegantly dressed people who were entering it.

"Everyone looks so beautiful, don't they?" Kitty said to Georgiana.

"Yes, they do," Georgiana agreed, "like butterflies fluttering in the night sky."

"Are we both being poetic?" Kitty returned. "And we haven't even had our first dance yet."

When we entered, we finally removed our cloaks and the gentlemen saw our gowns.

"Finally!" Mr. Darcy gasped. "I am able to marvel at your beauty. Dearest and loveliest Elizabeth, you are the handsomest woman that I have ever beheld."

"I will not be happy until I have danced with you." I deepened my voice to sound like him. "Although you dislike the amusement in general. After all, any savage can dance."

"Oh, be quiet you!" he teased, offering me his arm.

"Never, sir! I must give you pain, or else I will not be a proper fiancée."

Colonel Fitzwilliam, Mr. Bingley and Mr. Hurst also complimented all of us, and their compliments were mutual. For we declared them to look handsome as well.

Except Mr. Darcy and Miss Bingley (for it would not have been proper to do otherwise), all the other men in our group requested to dance with all of us.

"I am perfectly amenable to accepting any gentleman after the first two dances," Elena announced. "I promised the first two sets to someone else."

"Oh, and who is the fortunate cur?" Mr. Hurst asked.

"Sir Aleck Granger."

"And speak his name, and he shall appear," Sir Aleck said, coming up to us.

"Sir Aleck is everywhere, I cannot help but wonder," I retorted.

"I only wish I was omnipresent," he replied. "For in that way, I can look on the beauty of your company always. Ladies, if I may be so bold, you all are the most enchanting thing, putting even the pavilion to shame."

"How shall we live up to such a compliment?" Elena asked.

"You do not even have to try. You have already succeeded."

Taking her hand, he led her to the dance floor.

I danced with Mr. Darcy.

Mr. Bingley danced with Jane. (Of course, the Colonel secured her hand for the next set)

Colonel Fitzwilliam danced with Kitty.

Mr. Hurst danced with his wife.

Miss Bingley and Georgiana intended to sit out the first dance, but Mr. Dalton asked Georgiana to dance, and his cousin asked Miss Bingley.

Standing up together, the music began, and we all began to enjoy ourselves immensely.

"What are you feeling?" Mr. Darcy asked me.

"I'm feeling overwhelmed by your influence. Is this your life? All this grandeur and elegance? I wish that I could make you see things through my eyes, and you would glimpse the adventure that you have led us on. I didn't choose you because you would deliver me to this life. I chose you because I was comfortable around you. Because when I spoke, you would listen. And when you speak, I like to hear you."

"You were the first person who saw my words before you saw my name. I owe you everything for that."

"Would it be terrible for me to admit that I began to find you handsome as well?"

He raised one eyebrow.

"There is nothing wrong with finding one's spouse attractive," he said. "I daresay that one should do that. You are beautiful. The Royal Pavilion has seen little else as lovely."

"You had better be willing to dance with me again."

"That is an order that I am willing to obey."

The dance was proving to be a pleasure for all of us. I dare say that it helped that all of us went into it with no expectations for anything else but for what it was.

And for that, what a great contrast that it was to the Netherfield Ball!

I recalled, with unease, how much I had looked forward to dancing with Mr. Wickham, and to be cast down when he proved not to be there. Then I was forced to dance with Mr. Collins for an hour. And when I did dance with Mr. Darcy, I was out of spirits and spoke about things that caused him pain. The entire evening was splendid for Jane, who was wildly in love with Mr. Bingley at the time.

But for me, it had been nothing but a disappointment!

Although, this was the reverse. I had little time to prepare for this ball, I knew almost no one there, and yet, it was delightful. Miss Bingley had no reason to warn me about Mr. Wickham, I was engaged to the man that I loved, my mother was not there to embarrass us, Mary was not present to *sing*, and Lydia was not there to encourage Kitty's rambunctious side. Also, Mr. Hurst even asked me to dance, and he proved to be delightful company. After all, there was no agenda between us. Therefore, he had nothing to lose by being congenial.

And that gave me time to do what I wished: observe everyone.

For there were differences to this evening that were more than myself.

Jane's affections were split between two men now. Whatever pain it caused them, no one showed it. She was happy when speaking with both of them, and they refused to be jealous. It made me admire both men all the more.

Miss Bingley, who had once been next to Mr. Darcy at a ball, now was nowhere near him.

Sir Aleck and Elena looked similar to how Jane and Mr. Bingley looked at Netherfield. Unless he proved to be a rattle or rake, I declared that perhaps Sir Aleck really was in love with Elena.

Kitty's transformation was perhaps the largest. Being so close to Georgiana gave everyone the impression that she was a lovely woman, and so her reputation was very different than when at Netherfield. Men were eager to dance with her, and Kitty was willing. But there was something more. I believe, being tossed in love, then jilted, and then having to recover, may have done her good. Before that, she had never learned pain and hurt. Now that she had, she was no longer young in the ways of the world. Recovering from tragedy can alter a person's character, for we become aware of our own traits. If Kitty was broken within, she was constantly repairing herself. Somehow, it added to her beauty.

The chief triumph for her was that she was asked to dance with Mr. Dalton, who was our host.

Eventually, when we all sat down to eat dinner, Mr. Dalton asked Kitty and Georgiana to sit next to him. This compliment was eagerly accepted, and Sir Aleck took Georgiana's arranged seat near us, placing himself alongside Elena.

"Besotted," Mrs. Hurst said to me. "An excellent match. For he is rich, and she is handsome."

"You may speak of it freely, but I admit that I am afraid of saying anything," I acknowledged. "I fear that I will bring bad luck to it by expecting it. So, come what may. Though I wish that she receives the best of fortunes."

Suddenly, Mr. Dalton stood up and tapped his glass.

"Everyone, I might have fallen on a different sort of entertainment. There are many accomplished ladies present, and it puts me in a great desire for a song. However, afterwards, I might also be able to entice a writer to stand up and read something that she has written. Miss Darcy here is known for being one of the best musicians at the pianoforte, and she has agreed to perform. Yet, Miss Kitty here, has confessed to me that she is a writer. She has a great desire to write novels."

This announcement stirred the whole room, and everyone began to talk. I turned to Mr. Darcy, who looked concerned.

"What do you think everyone is saying?" I asked him.

"That it is not correct for women to write," he whispered. "I worried about Kitty being defamed for her industrious side. I wonder what Mr. Dalton is about."

"And" Mr. Dalton continued, "I have always had an appreciation for female writers. If there is one avenue that women have every right to be heard as much as us men, it is with writing. Do we not all agree?"

Everyone looked around at themselves, humbled by this. Whatever aspersions they were about to cast on my sister, now they might have been too embarrassed to.

I looked at Kitty, who was surprised at Mr. Dalton saying any of this.

"Miss Catherine Bennet told me that she was reading some of her writing on the way over here, in her carriage."

Everyone laughed at this.

"And, I have been curious to hear what this writing was like. To convince Miss Bennet, can we all give any sort of cheer? By doing so, I believe that she will feel obligated to entertain us. So, what of it, Miss Catherine Bennet? Will you read us some of your pages?"

Everyone clapped at this. Miss Kitty blushed, then she whispered something to Mr. Dalton. His expression showed that he was successful.

"She has agreed!" Mr. Dalton declared. Everyone cheered for this. "While Miss Kitty's papers are being retrieved from the carriage that she came in, Miss Darcy will entertain us."

Once more, everyone clapped at this. Georgiana walked over to the pianoforte and began to play. Her skill was masterful, and it cast a spell on everyone.

When she finished, everyone clapped eagerly.

Upon her completion, Georgiana sat down, and Kitty's papers had been retrieved.

"I am so scared for her now," I whispered.

"So am I," Mr. Darcy admitted.

And by the looks of it, so did Kitty. Standing up, in front of the room, Kitty was trembling.

"First," she said, her voice raised, "can everyone hear me?"

People laughed politely.

"My apologies if you cannot. Also, I will not deny that nothing I do will rise to the occasion of the excellent music that Miss Darcy has played for you all. She is my superior in every way, and well... now for something altogether different and I daresay—strange."

Kitty raised up the paper and began to read.

'Vanity & Vexations'
A Comedy of Errors

There has never been a rule set down that love must always be similar. Often, it is regarded as such by the minds of many who believe it to be a simple emotion that spawns one simple outcome. And if one is very fortunate, that love will lead to marriage. There! I have answered the answer for all: singularity is the format for love... until such a universal law becomes proven false, as all generalizations must give way to exceptions.

And perhaps, in some cases, it is best if it were not so, or no one would attempt to fall in love again after the first love was lost. There! I have set down a universal contradiction: no love is the same!

This was the fate of Mrs. Sarah Wellington. She had outlived her first husband, who passed away two years into their wedded bliss—or wedded horror. However, you wish to view that marriage is entirely to the freedom of those who read this. For, where the first marriage was made out of love and affection, it soon gave way to indifference on the husband's side and resentment on the lady's. There, that was the first of her loves! A passionate attachment that gave way to a series of contradictions. It was not till her husband died that she even remembered that she loved him to begin with.

Her life could have been frightening, for when a woman becomes a widow, she loses her chief protector. Returning to her family was not a bane to Mrs. Wellington, but she worried about being considered a burden to her parents, who never said she was, but the implications were always present.

Yet, love is not a singular thing, as has been established. Although, when it comes to England, love is not always fashionable at certain times of the year.

When seeing Mrs. Wellington, a certain gentleman did not care. His name was Mr. Frederick Gibson, and he had the most irrational encounter with love. He admired her from the very beginning of seeing her. Wondering if she could love again, Mrs. Wellington was hesitant to accept his affections. Also, married life, which had been so promising a thing, had not suited her as well as she had hoped. Eventually, she gave way, learned to feel a passionate attachment to him, and entered a second sort of love: a love that was created over time. Thus, she became Mrs. Sarah Gibson, and was the better for it. Her second match had the benefit of her being more experienced in love, him having a greater knowledge of the world than her first match, and them being wholly happy.

Mrs. Gibson had learned the plurality of life.

And that life gave her five daughters and no sons.

When hearing this, the crowd couldn't contain their awe. Five daughters alone is enough to make anyone gasp, but having no sons to shield this blow is altogether overwhelming. We knew; we lived it.

Happy that they were reacting, Kitty continued to read.

Marianne was the eldest, next was Isabella, Ruth, Cynthia and lastly was Rebecca. All five sisters had five distinct personalities and five very different sorts of beauty that required five different men with five different tastes.

In Hampshire, there is little room for a woman to become a heroine. Try as she might, believe as she may, but there is no place for trials, adventures and sometimes, love is not in season there either.

A young lady must sometimes go out into the world to have the adventure that will define her. Some women do this by choice, and others by obligation. All five sisters didn't need to choose: their adventure was thrust upon them one painful day.

Mr. Gibson, who had been the main doctor in the county, had done all in his power to have a son, and lived his life in torment that his daughters would have no one to protect them when he passed away. His daughters were never in want of affection of attention in life, for their parents had hearts that were large enough between them. This led to him being determined to live as long as he could. But they were county folk, with very little chance of any eligible gentlemen crossing their path, so when Mr. Gibson was thrown from his horse one day, he was rushed home and immediately had his wife write a letter to his relatives, imploring them to look after his widow and daughters, now that he was not there to shield them from the world.

Thus was the day that Marianne, Isabella, Ruth, Cynthia, and Rebecca had adventure thrust upon them. The day their father died marked the day that they would lose their home to a distant male heir. They had to send out inquiries to find a place to earn their living, while also refusing to be separated from their mother.

But should it be set down that a woman's prospects of romance should end when her life changes thus? And that is the question that this tale shall tell.

Five Gibson sisters had their situation, and thus had the path that was chosen for them. But could England supply five different sorts of men and contain five different sorts or loves?

For love, as we have established, is not a singular thing indeed.

When lowering the paper, everyone stared. In truth, I believe that they had been listening to every word that she said.

"That is all that I shall trouble you all with hearing," Kitty said.

We all laughed and the whole dining hall cheered for her.

"It was brilliant," Jane exclaimed. "It actually has the potential to be very good."

"Yes, so it would seem." I sighed, so very relieved that Kitty had been quite the triumph.

Food was brought out, we all began to eat, and soon it was discovered that we Bennet sisters really were five in number. Soon, we Bennets became the talk of the ball and of how much inspiration Kitty got from us. Surprisingly, we were not affronted by this, but only flattered.

Altogether, the evening went well, and we didn't leave until 2 o'clock in the morning.

When we departed, we were so exhausted that we fell asleep in the carriage.

# CHAPTER 19

## A TALK BETWEEN TWO MEN

Colonel Fitzwilliam departed from the ball with his company, and went back to Old Ship Hotel, tired and content.

He may not have had Jane Bennet's hand in marriage, but he had the next best thing, which was that Jane Bennet was not engaged to anyone else.

Since he would have to be called away to London to see to his regiment in two days, he knew very well that Mr. Bingley could press his advantage when he was gone. But more and more, he was accepting the fact that perhaps, in the end, Mr. Bingley was better for her. The ball cemented this. For while she was there, she was beautiful, was much admired, and it was a life that Mr. Bingley could give her—but he couldn't.

Yet this was something that he refused to vex himself over just yet. Right now, he would sleep in peace, grateful that he didn't have to wake up early the next day.

Unfortunately, fate had other things in store. At five o'clock in the morning, there was a knock on his door. It was an officer who told him that Mr. Joseph Martin was begging to speak to him, on a very grave matter that affected the Bennets.

Though exhausted, Colonel Fitzwilliam was a man of action and he quickly clothed, then left and went to where Mr. Martin was. In a medical room that was set up for him to recover from his wounds from punishment, Mr. Martin was recovering.

When Colonel Fitzwilliam entered, Mr. Martin began to appeal to him immediately.

"Colonel," he began, "forgive me for rousing you so early. But I have it upon good authority that an officer in Colonel Forster's regiment might be undergoing an elopement."

"What?"

"Yes. And her name is Miss Lydia Bennet."

This revelation forced Colonel Fitzwilliam to fully wake up immediately.

"Miss Lydia Bennet? You know this for certain?"

"It was something that I heard when I first came here. You may recall that I was looking at Miss Elizabeth Bennet oddly when I met her, and I asked if she was related to Miss Lydia. I heard from sources that an officer was wooing her and joked about how he could elope with her if he wished. At first, I passed it off as idle gossip. But, in my desire to make amends for my past mistakes, I had friends of mine keep abreast of new developments. It turns out that this officer has debts here in Brighton, and he is planning to flee before he must pay them. This officer boasted that he will not be alone when he flees."

"Joseph, tell me quickly! Who is this man?"

"Mr. George Wickham."

When hearing the name, Colonel Fitzwilliam grew irate.

"Him?" he spat. "Why does it always have to be him! I must leave you now."

"I understand," Mr. Martin said. "Just please, tell Miss Elena that I did this for you all. I want her to have one good memory of me."

"I will tell her. I can assure you. How is your back?"

Mr. Martin gestured to where the whip marks were.

"The worst part is over."

Colonel Fitzwilliam left Mr. Martin and immediately went to Colonel Forster's quarters. When inquiries became made, Mr. Martin proved to be correct. Mr. Wickham would prove to have eloped with Miss Lydia after all.

# CHAPTER 20

## THE MORNING AFTER

*I* woke up to a frantic banging at my door.

"Lizzy?" Jane said, rubbing her eyes. "Are there any candles near you?"

"I've got it," I said, getting a candle, lighting it, and going to the door. Opening it, Mr. Darcy was looking down at me, his face harsh. "Mr. Darcy?"

"I must enter," he said, "because I have to appraise you of some news that cannot be mentioned out here in the hall."

"Jane, Mr. Darcy is coming in."

"I understand," Jane said, putting a shawl around herself. "Mr. Darcy, what is it?"

"I come to tell you that I must leave immediately."

"Leave." I gasped, closing the door behind me. "Darcy, why?"

"Because I have not a moment to lose. I am going to London with the Colonel, for Lydia has eloped."

Jane and I were overwhelmed.

"What?" I exclaimed.

"Yes. She eloped early this morning, with Mr. Wickham."

I closed my eyes and Jane sat down, overcome.

"No, no, no," I moaned. "Is all really quite certain?"

"It is. Lizzy, I am sorry, but the Colonel is waiting for me. If we leave now, we can get them back. I know where he is headed. Believe me, I know where to find him."

"I must dress so that I can see you off," I rushed out.

"No, you mustn't," he said. "I wish for you to, but I must leave now. Look after my sister and Elena. And tell Mr. Bingley that I shall return soon. He will see to you all. Lizzy, please stay safe when I am away."

"Same with you. Do nothing to endanger yourself," I pleaded, "and please come back to me. I love you."

We kissed passionately.

"And I love you," he echoed. With one last longing look, he dashed down the hall. I watched him as he left, then I ran to the window and looked down at it. In front of the hotel, Colonel Fitzwilliam was on horseback, with a horse next to his. I saw Mr. Darcy emerge out of the hotel and mount the second stead.

Jane followed me at the window and looked down at them.

I pressed my hand to my heart. "And they will ride out of our lives."

"They will come back," Jane said. "They will be well."

"We don't know that," I said, tears clogging my throat. "We do not know that."

Both men rode away, to seek our fallen sister.

Jane and I clung to each other. "Jane," I sighed, "I am so terrified."

"So am I," she admitted. "So am I."

<br>

## End of Book III

<br>

Coming Fall 2022
*Chance Encounter Book 4*
*Chances End*

Don't miss out on your next favorite book!

Join the Satin Romance mailing list
www.satinromance.com/mail.html

# THANK YOU FOR READING

Did you enjoy this book?

We invite you to leave a review at your favorite book site, such as Goodreads, Amazon, Barnes & Noble, etc.

## DID YOU KNOW THAT LEAVING A REVIEW…

- Helps other readers find books they may enjoy.
- Gives you a chance to let your voice be heard.
- Gives authors recognition for their hard work.
- Doesn't have to be long. A sentence or two about why you liked the book will do.

# ABOUT THE AUTHOR

**Ney Mitch** has been a long-standing Jane Austen enthusiast, having written forty novels that were inspired by her various works. Since stumbling on Miss Austen's books after graduating from college, she has always dabbled in Austen inspired literature, ranging from writing works for teens to adults. Originally, her desire was to adapt Jane Austen's writing in a way to help young adults connect with her, however over time, she has spread her aims to other genres and styles. Having received her BA Degree at Desales University, she is a writer, both literary and dramatic, as well as being a Historic Reenactor.

 facebook.com/courtney.mitchell.589

 twitter.com/CMMitchelPsyche

pinterest.com/shebaanna